CAPTAIN ALATRISTE

ARTURO PÉREZ-REVERTE

Translated from the Spanish by
Margaret Sayers Peden

Weidenfeld & Nicolson

LONDON

First published in Great Britain in 2005
by Weidenfeld & Nicolson

3 5 7 9 10 8 6 4 2

A CIP catalogue record for this book
is available from the British Library.

ISBN 0 297 84846 1

Printed in Great Britain by Clays Ltd, St Ives plc

Weidenfeld & Nicolson

The Orion Publishing Group Ltd
Orion House
5 Upper St Martin's Lane
London, WC2H 9EA

www.orionbooks.co.uk

For our grandparents Sebastián, Amelia, Pepe, and Cala:
for life, books and memories

Was once a captain
The story goes
Who led men in battle
Though in death's throes.
Oh, señores! What an apt man
was that brave captain!

E. MARQUINA
The Sun Has Set in Flanders

CAPTAIN ALATRISTE

I. THE TAVERN OF THE TURK

He was not the most honest or pious of men, but he was courageous. His name was Diego Alatriste y Tenorio, and he had fought in the ranks during the Flemish wars. When I met him he was barely making ends meet in Madrid, hiring himself out for four *maravedís* in employ of little glory, often as a swordsman for those who had neither the skill nor the daring to settle their own quarrels. You know the sort I mean: a cuckolded husband here, outstanding gambling debts there, a petty lawsuit or questionable inheritance, and more troubles of that kind. It is easy to criticize now, but in those days the capital of all the Spains was a place where a man had to fight for his life on a street corner lighted by the gleam of two blades.

In all this Diego Alatriste played his part with panache. He showed great skill when swords were drawn, even more when with left-handed cunning he wielded the long, narrow dagger some call the *vizcaína*, a weapon from Biscay that professionals often used to help their cause along. If a knife will not do it, the *vizcaína* will, was the old saying. The adversary would be concentrating on attacking and parrying, and suddenly, quick as lightning, with one upward slash, his gut would be slit, so fast he would not have time to ask for confession. Oh yes, Your Mercies, those were indeed harsh times.

Captain Alatriste, as I was saying, lived by his sword. Until I came into the picture, that "Captain" was more an honorary title than a true rank. His nickname originated one night when, serving as a soldier in the king's wars, he had to cross an icy river with twenty-nine companions and a true captain. Imagine, *Viva España* and all that, with his sword clenched between his teeth, and in his shirtsleeves to blend into the snow, all to surprise a Hollandish contingent. They were the enemy at the time because they were fighting for independence. In fact, they did win it in the end, but meanwhile we gave them a merry chase.

Getting back to the captain—the plan was to stay there on the riverbank, or dike, or whatever the devil it was, until dawn, when the troops of our lord and king would launch an attack and join them. To make a long story short, the heretics were duly dispatched without time for a last word.

They were sleeping like marmots when our men emerged from the icy water, nearly frozen, shaking off the cold by speeding heretics to Hell, or wherever it is those accursed Lutherans go. What went wrong is that the dawn came, and the morning passed, and the expected Spanish attack did not materialize. A matter, they told later, of old jealousies among the generals and officers in the field. Fact is, thirty-one men were abandoned to their fate, amid curses and vows, surrounded by Low Dutch disposed to avenge the slashed throats of their comrades. With less chance than the Invincible Armada of the good King Philip the Second.

It was a long and very hard day. And in order that Your Mercies may picture what happened, only two of the Spanish made it back to the other bank of the river by the time night fell. Diego Alatriste was one of them, and as all day long he had commanded the troops—the authentic captain having been rendered hors de combat in the first skirmish with two handspans of steel protruding from his back—the title fell to him, though he had no opportunity to enjoy the honor. Captain-for-a-day of troops fated to die, and paying their way to Hell at the cost of their hides, one after another, with the river to their backs and blaspheming in good Castilian Spanish. But that is the way of war and the maelstrom. That is the way it goes with Spain.

Well, then. My father was the other Spanish soldier

who returned that night. His name was Lope Balboa; he was from the province of Guipuzcoa, and he, too, was a courageous man. They say that Diego Alatriste and he were very good friends, almost like brothers, and it must be true, because later, on the bulwarks of Julich, where my father was killed by a ball from a harquebus—which was why Diego Velázquez did not include him in his painting of the Surrender of Breda, as he did his friend and fellow Diego, Alatriste, who is indeed there, behind the horse—he swore that he would look after me when I grew out of childhood. And that is why, when I turned thirteen, my mother supplied me with shirt and breeches, and a rosary and a crust of bread tied up in a kerchief, and sent me to live with the captain, taking advantage of a cousin who was traveling to Madrid. Thus it was that I came to enter the service, at a rank somewhere between servant and page, of my father's friend.

A confidence: I very much doubt whether, had she known him well, the mother who gave me birth would so gaily have sent me to his service. But I suppose that the title of captain, though apocryphal, added sheen to his character. Besides, my poor mother was not well and she had two daughters to feed. By sending me off she had one fewer mouth at table and at the same time was giving me the opportunity to seek my fortune at court. So, without bothering to ask further details, she packed me off with her cousin, together with a long letter written by the priest of our town, in which she reminded Diego Alatriste of his promise and his friendship with my deceased father.

I recall that when I attached myself to the captain, not much time had passed since his return from Flanders, because he carried an ugly wound in his side received at Fleurus, still fresh, and the source of great pain. Newly arrived, timid, and as easily frightened as a mouse, on my pallet at night I would listen to him pace back and forth in his room, unable to sleep. And at times I heard him softly singing little verses, interrupted by stabs of pain: Lope's verses, then a curse or a comment to himself, partly resigned and almost amused. That was typical of the captain: to face each of his ills and misfortunes as if they were a kind of inevitable joke that an old, perverse acquaintance found entertaining to subject him to from time to time. Perhaps that was the origin of his peculiar sense of harsh, unchanging, despairing humor.

That was a long time ago, and I am a bit muddled regarding dates. But the story I am going to tell you must have taken place around sixteen hundred and twenty-something. It is the adventure of masked men and two Englishmen, which caused not a little talk at court, and in which the captain not only came close to losing the patched-up hide he had managed to save in Flanders, and in battling Turkish and Barbary corsairs, but also made himself a pair of enemies who would harass him for the rest of his life. I am referring to the secretary of our lord and king, Luis de Alquézar, and to his sinister Italian assassin, the silent and dangerous swordsman named Gualterio Malatesta, a man so accustomed to killing his victims from behind that when by chance he faced them, he sank into deep depressions, imagining that he was losing his touch. It was also the year in which I fell in love like a bawling calf, then and forever, with Angélica de Alquézar, who was as perverse and wicked as only Evil in the form of a blonde eleven- or twelve-year-old girl can be. But we will tell everything in its time.

My name is Íñigo. And my name was the first word Captain Alatriste uttered the morning he was released from the ancient prison in the castle, where he had spent three weeks as a guest of the king for nonpayment of debts. That he was the king's "guest" is merely a manner of speaking, for in this as in other prisons of the time, the only luxuries—and food was included as such—were those a prisoner paid for from his own purse. Fortunately, although the captain had been incarcerated nearly innocent of any funds, he had a goodly number of friends. So thanks to one and then another fellow who came to his aid during his imprisonment, his stay was made more tolerable by the stews that Caridad la Lebrijana, the mistress of the Tavern of the Turk, sometimes sent by way of me, and by the four *reales* sent by his companions don Francisco de Quevedo and Juan Vicuña, among others.

As for the rest of it, and here I am referring to the hardships of prison life itself, the captain knew better than any how to protect himself. The practice of relieving one's wretched companions-in-misfortune of their wealth, clothes, even their shoes, was notorious at that time. But Diego Alatriste was quite well known in Madrid, and any who did not know him soon found it was better for their health to approach him with caution. According to what I later learned, the first thing he did, once inside the walls, was to go straight to the most dangerous ruffian among the prisoners and, after greeting him politely, press the cold blade of that lethal *vizcaína*—which he had kept thanks to the transfer of a few *maravedís* to the jailer—to the thug's gullet. It worked like a sign from God. After this unmistakable declaration of principles, no one dared lift a hand against the captain, who from then on slept in peace, wrapped in his cape in a reasonably clean corner of the establishment and protected by his reputation as a man with steel in his spine.

Later, his generous sharing of La Lebrijana's stews, as well as bottles of wine bought from the warden with the assistance of friends, helped secure him solid loyalties, even from the lowlife of that first day, a man from Córdoba with the unfortunate name of Bartolo Cagafuego. Although carrying the burden of a name like Bartolo Shitfire was reason enough to get him into trouble as regularly as a pious old dame goes to mass—and though he had spent more than his share of time in the king's galleys—he was not a rancorous fellow. It was one of Diego Alatriste's virtues that he could make friends in Hell.

It seems unreal. I do not remember the exact year— it was the twenty-second or twenty-third year of the century—but what I am sure of is that the captain emerged from the prison on one of those blue, luminous Madrid mornings so cold that it takes your breath away. From that day—though neither of us yet knew it—our lives were going to change greatly.

Time has gone by and water has flowed beneath the bridges of the Manzanares, but I can still see Diego Alatriste, thin and unshaven, stepping across the threshold with the heavy iron-studded door closing behind him. I recall him perfectly, squinting in the blinding light, thick mustache covering his upper lip, slim silhouette wrapped in his cape, and beneath the shadow of his wide-brimmed hat, bedazzled eyes that seemed to smile when he glimpsed me sitting on a bench in the plaza. There was something very unusual about the captain's gaze; on the one hand, his eyes were very clear and very cold, a greenish-gray like the water in puddles on a winter morning. On the other, they could suddenly break into a warm and welcoming smile, like a blast of heat melting a skim of ice, while the rest of his face remained serious, inexpressive, or grave. He had another, more disturbing, smile that he reserved for moments of danger or sadness: a kind of grimace that twisted his mustache down slightly toward the left corner of his mouth, a smile as threatening as cold steel—which nearly always followed—or as funereal as an omen of death when it was strung at the end of several bottles of wine, those the captain dispatched alone in his days of silence. The first one or two downed without taking a breath, then that gesture of wiping his mustache with the back of his hand while staring at the wall before him. Bottles to kill the ghosts, he always said, although he was never able to kill them completely.

The smile he directed at me that morning when he found me waiting belonged to the first category: the one that lighted his eyes, refuting the imperturbable gravity of his face and the harshness he often intentionally gave to his words, even when he was far from feeling it. He looked up and down the street, appeared to be satisfied when he did not see any new creditor lurking about, walked toward me, removed his cape, despite the cold, and tossed it to me, wadded into a ball.

"Íñigo," he said. "Boil this. It is crawling with bedbugs."

The cape stunk, as did he. His clothing held enough bugs to chew the ear off a bull, but all that was resolved less than an hour later in Mendo el Toscano's bathhouse. A native of Tuscany, the barber had been a soldier in Naples when only a lad, and he admired Diego Alatriste greatly, and trusted him. When I arrived with a change of clothing—the only other full outfit the captain kept in the battered old cupboard that served us as a clothespress—I found him standing in a wood tub overflowing with dirty water, drying himself. El Toscano had trimmed his beard for him, and the short, wet chestnut hair combed back and parted in the middle revealed a broad forehead tanned by the sun of the prison courtyard but marred by a small scar that ran down to his left eyebrow. As he finished drying and putting on the clean breeches and shirt, I observed other scars I was already familiar with. One in the shape of a half-moon between his navel and his left nipple. A long one that zigzagged down a thigh. Both had been made by a cutting blade, a sword or dagger, unlike a fourth on his back, which had formed the telltale star left by a musket ball. The fifth was the most recent, still not completely healed, the one that kept him from sleeping well every night: a violet gash almost a hand's breadth wide on his left side, a souvenir of the battle of Fleurus. It was months old, and at times it opened and oozed pus, although that day as its owner stepped out of the tub it did not look too bad.

I helped him as he dressed, slowly and carelessly: dark gray doublet and knee breeches of the same color, tight at the knees over the buskins that hid the ladders in his hose. Then he buckled on the leather belt that I had carefully oiled during his absence, and into it thrust the sword with the large quillons, whose blade and guard showed the nicks, knocks, and scratches of other days and other blades. It was a good sword, long, intimidating, and of the best Toledo steel, and as it was drawn or sheathed it gave off a long metallic *sssssss* that would give you gooseflesh. He studied his reflection in a dim half-length mirror for a moment, and smiled a weary smile.

" 'Sblood," he muttered, "I feel thirsty."

Without another word he preceded me down the stairs and along Calle Toledo toward the Tavern of the Turk. As he had no cloak, he walked along the sunny side, head high, with the frazzled red plume in the band of his hat dipping and waving. He touched his hand to the wide brim to greet some acquaintance, or swept the hat off as he passed a lady of a certain status. I followed, distracted, taking in everything: the urchins playing in the street, the vegetable vendors in the arcades, and the groups of gossiping idlers sitting in the sun beside the Jesuit church. Although I had never been overly innocent, and the months I had been living in the neighborhood had had the virtue of opening my eyes, I was still a young and curious

ARTURO PÉREZ-REVERTE

pup who looked at the world with an astonished gaze, trying not to miss a single detail.

As for the carriage, all I noticed at first were the hoofbeats of a team of mules and the sound of wheels approaching behind us. I scarcely paid attention; seeing coaches and carriages was a normal occurrence, because the street was the principal route to the Plaza Mayor and the castle, the Alcázar Real. But when I looked up for an instant as the carriage caught up to us, I saw a door without a shield and, in the small window, the face of a girl with blond hair combed into corkscrew curls, and the bluest, clearest, and most unsettling eyes I have ever seen. Those eyes met mine for an instant, and then the enchanting creature was borne off down the street.

I shuddered, not knowing why. But my shudder would have been even stronger had I known that I had just been gazed upon by the Devil.

"We have no choice but to fight," said don Francisco de Quevedo.

The table was littered with empty bottles, and every time that don Francisco was a little too liberal with the wine of San Martín de Valdeiglesias—which happened frequently—he was ready to call out Christ himself.

Quevedo was slightly lame, a poet, a fancier of whores, nearsighted, and a Caballero de Santiago. He was as quick with his wit and his tongue as with his sword, and he was famous at court for his good poems and bad temper. The latter was, all too often, the cause for his wandering from exile to exile and prison to prison. It is well known that though, like all of Madrid, our good lord and king, Philip the Fourth, and his favored Conde de Olivares appreciated the poet's satiric verses, the king liked much less being the subject of them. So from time to time, after the appearance of some sonnet or anonymous poem in which everyone recognized the poet's hand, the magistrate's bailiffs and constables would swarm into the tavern, or Quevedo's domicile, or a place where friends met to exchange gossip, to invite him, respectfully, to accompany them, taking him out of circulation for a few days or months. As he was stubborn and proud, and never learned his lesson, these occurrences were numerous, and served to embitter him.

Quevedo was, nevertheless, an excellent table companion and a good friend to his friends, among whom he included Captain Alatriste. Both went often to the Tavern of the Turk, where they would gather their friends around one of the best tables, which Caridad la Lebrijana—who had been a whore and still was occasionally for the captain, though free of charge—usually reserved for them. That morning, along with don Francisco and the captain, the group was completed by habitués: Licenciado Calzas, Juan Vicuña, Dómine Pérez, and El Tuerto Fadrique, the one-eyed apothecary at the Puerta Cerrada.

"No choice but to fight," the poet insisted.

He was, as I have said, visibly "illuminated" by a bottle or two of Valdeiglesias. He had jumped to his feet, overturning a taboret, and with his hand resting on the pommel of his sword, was sending blazing glances toward the occupants of a nearby table. There, two strangers, whose long swords and capes were hanging on the wall, had just congratulated the poet on a few verses. Unfortunately, those lines actually had been written by Luis de Góngora, Quevedo's most despised adversary in the Republic of Letters—a rival whom, among other insults, he accused of being a sodomite, a dog, and a Jew. The newcomers had spoken in good faith, or at least it seemed so, but don Francisco was not disposed to overlook their words.

> "*I shall grease my poems with the fat of the pig*
> *So that gnat Góngora cannot chew off a piece. . . .*"

He began to improvise there on the spot, weaving a little, hand still clutching the hilt of his sword, while the strangers tried to apologize and the captain and his table companions held on to don Francisco to keep him from drawing his sword and going for the offenders.

"But by God, that is an insult," the poet cried, trying to loose the right hand his friends were gripping so tightly, while with his free hand he adjusted his twisted eyeglasses. "A bit of steel will make things, *hic*, right."

"That is too much steel to squander so early in the day, don Francisco," Diego Alatriste sensibly interceded.

"It seems very little to me." Without taking his eyes off his perceived tormentors, the poet ferociously smoothed his mustache. "But we will be generous: one hand's breadth of steel for each of these *hijosdalgo*, who are sons of something, no doubt, but very certainly not sons of hidalgos."

These were fighting words, so the strangers made as if to claim their swords and go outside. The captain and the other friends, helpless to prevent the confrontation, asked them please to make allowances for the poet's alcoholic state and simply quit the field, adding that there was no glory in fighting a drunk opponent, or shame in withdrawing prudently to prevent greater harm.

"*Bella gerant alii*," suggested Dómine Pérez, trying to temporize.

Dómine Pérez was a Jesuit priest who tended his flock in the nearby church of San Pedro y San Pablo. His kindly

nature and his Latin phrases tended to have a soothing effect, for he spoke them in a tone of unquestionable good
sense. The two strangers, however, knew no Latin, and the
insult of being called sonsofsomethingorother was difficult to brush off. Besides, the cleric's mediation was under-
cut by the scoffing banter of Licenciado Calzas, a clever,
cynical rascal who haunted the courts, a specialist in defending causes he could convert into endless trials that bled
his clients of their last *maravedís*. The *licenciado* loved to
stir things up, and he was always goading every Juan, José,
and Tomasillo.

"You do not want to lose face, don Francisco," he said
in a low voice. "They will pay the court costs, defend
your honor."

So all those gathered round prepared to witness an
event that would appear the next day in the sheets of *Avisos
y noticias*, the city's purveyor of notices and news. And
Captain Alatriste, failing in his efforts to calm his friend,
but knowing he would not leave don Francisco alone in
the fray, began to accept as inevitable that he would be
crossing swords with these strangers.

"Aio te vincere posse," Dómine Pérez concluded with
resignation, as Licenciado Calzas hid his laughter by snort-
ing into his jug of wine. With a deep sigh, the captain
started to get up from the table. Don Francisco, who al-

ready had drawn four fingers of his sword from its scabbard, shot him a comradely look of thanks, and even had the brass to direct a couplet to him.

"You, Diego, whose sword so nobly defends
The name and honor of your family . . ."

"Do not fuck with me, don Francisco," the captain replied ill-humoredly. "We will have our fight with whom we must, but do not fuck with me."

"That is how a true, *hic*, man talks," said the poet, visibly grateful for the friend who had just sworn his support. The rest of the gatherers unanimously urged him on, like Dómine Pérez, abandoning any conciliatory efforts and in truth delightedly anticipating the spectacle. For if don Francisco de Quevedo, particularly in his cups, turned out to be a terrible swordsman, the intervention of Diego Alatriste as his partner at the ball left no shred of doubt regarding the results. Bets flew about the number of thrusts the strangers would pay for.

So. The captain gulped a swallow of wine and, already on his feet, looked over toward the strangers as if to apologize that things had gone so far. He motioned with his head for them to step outside, in order not to destroy the tavern of Caridad la Lebrijana, who was always fretting about the furniture.

"Whenever Your Mercies please."

The men buckled on their weapons and started outside amid high expectation, taking care not to leave their backs unguarded—just in case—for Jesus may have said something about brothers, but he made no mention of cousins. That was the situation, with all swords still sheathed, when, to the disappointment of the onlookers and relief of Diego Alatriste, the unmistakable silhouette of the high constable, Martín Saldaña, appeared in the doorway.

"That throws the blanket over our fiesta," said don Francisco de Quevedo.

And shrugging, he adjusted his eyeglasses, glanced out of the corner of his eye, went back to his table, and uncorked another bottle, with no further ado.

"I have a mission for you."

The high constable, Martín Saldaña, was hard and tan as a brick. Over his doublet, he wore an old-fashioned buff-coat, quilted inside, that was very practical in warding off knives. With his sword, dagger, poniard, and pistols, he carried more iron than was to be found in all Biscay. He had been a soldier in the Flemish wars, like Diego Alatriste and my deceased father, and in close camaraderie with them had spent long years of pain and worry, although in the end with better fortune. While my progenitor pushed up daisies in a land of heretics, and the captain earned his living as a hired swordsman, Saldaña made his way in Madrid upon his discharge in Flanders—after our deceased king, Philip the Third, signed a treaty with the Dutch—with the help of a brother-in-law who was a majordomo in the palace, and a mature but still-beautiful wife. I cannot prove the story of the wife—I was too young to know the details—but there were rumors that a certain magistrate was free to have his way with the aforementioned señora, and that that was the reason for her husband's being appointed high constable, a position equal to that of the night watchmen who made their rounds in the barrios of Madrid, which at that time were still called *cuarteles*.

In any case, no one ever dared make the least insinuation in Martín Saldaña's presence. Cuckolded or not, there was no doubt was that he was brave, albeit very thin-skinned. He had been a good soldier; his many wounds had been stitched up like a crazy quilt, and he knew how to command respect with his fists or with a Toledo sword. He was, in fact, as honorable as could be expected in a high constable of the time. He, too, admired Diego Alatriste, and he tried to favor him whenever possible. Theirs was an old professional friendship—rough, as befitting men of their nature—but real and sincere.

"A mission," the captain repeated. They had gone outside and were leaning against a wall in the sun, each with his jug in his hand, watching people and carriages pass by on Calle Toledo. Saldaña looked at him a moment, stroking the thick beard sprinkled with the gray of an old soldier, grown to hide a slash that went from his mouth to his left ear.

"You have been out of prison only a few hours and you haven't a coin in your purse," he said. "Before two days pass, you will have accepted some paltry employ, escorting some conceited young peacock to prevent his beloved's brother from running him through on a street corner or slicing off a man's ears on behalf of a creditor. Or you will start hanging around in bawdy and gaming houses to see what you can extract from strangers or a priest who's come to wager San Eufrasio's knucklebone. Before you know it, you will be in trouble: a bad wound, a quarrel, a charge against you. And then it will start all over again." He took a small sip from his jar and half closed his eyes, though he never took them off the captain. "Do you call that living?"

Diego Alatriste shrugged. "Can you think of something better?" He stared directly into the eyes of his old comrade from Flanders. The look said, *We do not all have the good fortune to be a high constable.*

Saldaña picked his teeth with a fingernail and nodded a couple of times. They both knew that were it not for the twists and turns of fate, Saldaña could easily be in the same situation as the captain. Madrid was filled with former soldiers scraping a living in the streets and plazas, their belts stuffed with tin tubes in which they carried their wrinkled recommendations and petitions, and the useless service records that no one gave a fig about. Waiting for a stroke of luck that never came.

"That is why I have come, Diego. There is someone who needs you."

"Me? Or my sword?" He twisted his mustache with that grimace that passed as a smile.

Saldaña burst out laughing. "What an idiotic question," he said. "There are women who are interesting for their charms, priests for their absolutions, old men for their money. . . . As for men like you and me, it is only our swords." He paused to look in both directions, took another swallow of wine, and spoke more quietly. "These are people of quality. An easy evening's work, with no risks but the usual ones. And for doing it, there is a handsome purse."

The captain observed his friend with interest. At that moment, the word "purse" would have roused him from the deepest sleep or the most excruciating hangover.

"How 'handsome'?"

"Some sixty *escudos*. In good four-doubloon coins."

"Not bad." The pupils narrowed in Diego Alatriste's light eyes. "Is killing involved?"

Saldaña made an evasive gesture, looking furtively toward the door of the tavern.

"Perhaps, but I do not know the details. And I do not want to know, if you get my meaning. All I know is that it is to be an ambush. Something discreet, at night, with your face covered and all that. 'Greetings and godspeed, señores!'"

"Alone, or will I have company?"

"Company, I surmise. There are two to be dispatched. Or perhaps only given a good fright. Or maybe you can use your blade to leave the sign of the cross on their faces, or something of the kind. You will know what to do."

"Who are they?"

Now Saldaña shook his head, as if he had said more than he wanted. "Everything in its time. Besides, my only role is to act as messenger."

The captain drained his jug, thinking hard. In those days, fifteen four-doubloon pieces, in gold, came to more than seven hundred *reales*. Enough to get him out of difficulty, buy new linens and a suit of clothes, pay off his debts . . . set his life in order a little. Spruce up the two rented rooms where he and I lived on the upper floor of a courtyard behind the tavern, facing the Calle del Arcabuz. Eat hot food without depending on the generous thighs of Caridad la Lebrijana.

"And also," Saldaña added, seeming to follow the thread of the captain's thoughts, "this job will put you in contact with important people. Good for the future."

"My future," the captain echoed, absorbed in his thoughts.

II. THE MASKED MEN

The street was dark and there was not a soul to be seen. Swathed in an old cloak that don Francisco de Quevedo had lent him, Diego Alatriste stopped beside an adobe wall and took a cautious look around. A lamppost, Saldaña had said. In fact, a small lamp stood on a pole in the hollow of a postern gate; beyond it, through the branches of the trees, could be seen the dark roof tiles of a house.

It was the winding-down hour, near midnight, when the neighbors call out a warning, then empty their chamber pots out the windows, or hired cutthroats stalk their victims through the unlighted streets. But here there were no neighbors, nor did there seem ever to have been any; everything lay in silence. As for possible thieves and assassins, Diego Alatriste was prepared. At a very early age he had learned a basic principle of life and survival: If you are stout of heart, you can be as dangerous as anyone who crosses your path. Or more.

As for the appointment that night, the instructions said to take the first street to the right after the old Santa Bárbara gate, and walk on until coming to a brick wall and a light. So far, everything was going well. The captain stood quietly for a moment to look the place over, careful not to look directly at the lamp on the pole, so that it would not blind him and keep him from seeing into the darkest corners. Finally, after running his hands over the buffalo-hide buffcoat he had put on beneath his doublet in case of an untimely encounter with a knife, he pulled his hat lower and slowly walked toward the gate.

I had watched him dress with great care an hour earlier in our rooms.

"I will be late, Íñigo. Do not wait up."

We had dined on soup, with a few crumbs of bread, a small measure of wine, and two boiled eggs. Later, after washing his face and hands in a basin as I mended some ancient hose by the light of a tallow lamp, Diego Alatriste prepared to go out, taking all the necessary safeguards. It was not that he suspected a trick on the part of Martín Saldaña, but high constables themselves may be the victims of deceit . . . or be bribed. Including constables who are old friends and comrades. And had that been the case, Alatriste would not have been too resentful. In that day, anything within the ambit of the young, pleasant, womanizing, pious, and lethal-for-poor-all-the-Spains Philip the Fourth could be bought; even consciences. Not that things have changed that much since then.

In any case, the captain took every precaution on his way to the rendezvous. He tucked the *vizcaína* that had served him so well in the town prison into the back of his belt, and I saw him slip his short slaughterer's knife into his boot. As he made these preparations, I sneaked glances at his grave, absorbed face. The light from the tallow lamp deepened the hollow of his cheeks and accentuated the fierce line of his mustache. He did not seem very proud of himself. For a moment, as he looked about for his sword, his eyes met mine, and then instantly he looked away, his eyes avoiding mine, as if fearful that I would read something in them he did not want to reveal. But only for an instant, and then he looked straight at me again, with a quick, open smile.

"A man has to earn his bread, lad."

That was all he said. He buckled on the belt with the sword—he always refused, except in war, to sling it over his shoulder, as the common swaggering, strutting good-for-nothings did—testing to be sure that he could easily draw it from the scabbard, and donned the cloak he had borrowed from don Francisco that same afternoon. The cape, aside from the fact that we were in March and it was too cold at night to be without one, had another use: in that dangerous Madrid of narrow, badly lighted streets, the garment was very practical in a sword fight. Folded across the chest, or rolled around the left arm, it made a handy buckler for protecting oneself, and thrown over the adversary's sword, it hampered him long enough to get in a good blow. In the end, fighting a clean fight when risking one's hide might have contributed to the salvation of the soul in the life eternal, but insofar as life on this earth was concerned, it was doubtlessly the shortest path to giving up the ghost, and looking like a fool with a handspan of steel in one's liver. And Diego Alatriste was in no damned hurry to go.

The lamp shed an oily light on the postern gate. The captain knocked four times, as Saldaña had told him to do. That done, he freed the hilt of his sword and kept his left hand behind him, near the *vizcaína*. From the other side of the door he could hear footsteps. The door opened silently, and the silhouette of a servant filled the opening.

"Your name?"

"Alatriste."

Without a word, the retainer started off, preceding the captain along a path that wound through the trees of a garden. The building the captain was led to seemed abandoned. Although he did not know the part of Madrid near the Hortaleza road well, he fitted some pieces together and thought he could recall the walls and roof of a decrepit old house he had once glimpsed as he passed by.

"Wait here, Your Mercy, until they call for you."

Alatriste and his guide had just entered a small room with bare walls and no furniture, where the flickering light from a candelabrum set on the floor played over the old paintings on the wall. In one corner of the room stood a man muffled in a black cape; a wide-brimmed hat of the same color covered his head. He had not moved when the captain entered, and when the servant—who in the candle-light was revealed to be of middle age, and wearing livery that the captain could not identify—retired, leaving the two of them alone, he still stood motionless, like a dark sculpture, observing Alatriste. The only signs of life visible between the cape and the hat were dark, gleaming eyes, which the candlelight picked out among the shadows, lending their owner a menacing and ghostly air. With one experienced glance, Diego Alatriste noted the leather boots and the sword tip that slightly lifted the back of the man's cape. His aplomb was that of a professional swordsman, or a soldier.

Neither spoke; they merely stood there, still and silent, on either side of the candelabrum lighting them from below, studying each other to ascertain whether they found themselves in the company of a comrade or an adversary. Although in Diego Alatriste's profession, it could be both at the same time.

"I want no deaths," said the tall masked man.

He was heavy-bodied, broad in the shoulders, and he was also the only one who had not removed his hat, which had no plume, band, or adornment. Visible beneath the mask covering his face was the tip of a thick black beard. He was dressed in dark, fine-quality clothing, with cuffs and collar of Flemish lace, and beneath the cloak draped across his shoulders glinted a gold chain and the gilded pommel of a sword. He spoke as one accustomed to commanding and being immediately obeyed, and that was confirmed in the deference shown him by his masked companion, who was clad in a loose garment that concealed his attire. He was a man of medium stature, with a round head and thin hair. These two had received Diego Alatriste and the black-cloaked man after having made them wait half an hour in the antechamber.

"No deaths, no blood," the tall, corpulent one insisted. "At least, not much."

His companion raised both hands. Diego Alatriste observed that he had dirty fingernails and ink-stained fingers, like those of a scribe; however, a heavy gold seal ring encircled the little finger of his left hand.

"Perhaps just a pink," they heard him suggest in a prudent voice. "Something to justify the encounter."

"But only for the blonder of the two," the finely dressed man amplified.

"Of course, Excellency."

Alatriste and the man in the voluminous cape exchanged a professional glance, as if considering the bounds of the word "pink" and the possibilities—rather remote—of distinguishing one blond from another in the midst of a scuffle, and at night. Picture the scene: Would you be kind enough to come to the light and doff your hat? Thank you, caballero. I see that you are blonder than your friend. Please allow me to pierce your liver. . . . I'll use no more than a quarter of my blade.

In a pig's eye.

As for the man wrapped in the cloak, he had removed his hat when they entered the room, and now Alatriste could see his face in the light of the table lamp illuminating the four men and the walls of an old library thick with dust and nibbled by mice. He was tall, slender, silent, and around thirty years old. His face bore the old marks of smallpox, and the thin line of his mustache gave him the look of a stranger, a foreigner. His eyes and his hair, which fell to his shoulders, were as black as his clothing, and in his sash was a sword with an uncommonly large, round steel guard with exaggerated quillons. No one but a consummate swordsman would have dared expose such a weapon to the inevitable gibes and jeers unless he had the daring and dexterity to defend its oddity with deeds. And this man did not look like someone who would be a target for poking fun. If you looked up the words "swordsman" and "assassin," it was his portrait you would find.

"Your quarries, caballeros, are two foreign gentlemen," the round-headed man said. "They are traveling incognito, so that their real names and circumstances will exert no influence. The elder is called Thomas Smith, and he is no more than thirty. The other, John Smith, is nearly twenty-three. They will arrive in Madrid on horseback, alone, at night. Weary, I imagine, for they have been traveling for days. We do not know which gate they will enter by, so the best plan would seem to be to wait for them near their destination, which is the House of Seven Chimneys. Do you know it, Your Mercies?"

Diego Alatriste and his companion nodded. Everyone in Madrid knew the residence of the Count of Bristol, England's ambassador.

"This is the way the affair must go," the masked man continued. "It must look as if the two travelers were victims of an assault by common highwaymen. That means that you must take everything they are carrying with them. It would be helpful if the blonder and more arrogant, who is the elder, were slightly injured. A knife wound in a leg or arm, but nothing too serious. As for the younger, you can let him go with just a good fright." At this point, the man who was talking turned slightly toward the corpulent man, as if awaiting his approval. "It is important that you make off with any letters and documents they have, and deliver them punctually."

"To whom?" asked Alatriste.

"To someone who will be waiting on the other side of the Discalced Carmelite monastery. The countersign is *'Monteros y suizos.'*"

As he was speaking, the man with the round head put his hand inside the dark robes covering his clothing and removed a small purse. For an instant, Alatriste thought he glimpsed on his chest the bright red embroidery of the cross of the Order of Calatrava, but his attention was quickly diverted by the money the masked man put on the table. The lamplight reflected off five four-doubloon pieces for Alatriste's companion, and five for him. Clean, burnished coins. A powerful caballero, that money. Yes, this is what don Francisco de Quevedo would have said, had he been party to their conversation . . . powerful indeed.

Blessed coins, newly minted with the coat of arms of our lord and king. Bliss with which to buy bed, food, clothing, and the warmth of a woman.

"Ten pieces are missing," said the captain, "for each of us."

The other man's tone was instantly unpleasant. "The person who will be waiting for you tomorrow night will give you the rest, in exchange for the travelers' documents."

"And if something turns out badly?"

From the holes in his mask, the eyes of the heavyset man whom his companion had addressed as "Excellency" seemed to pierce the captain. "It would be best, for the well-being of all concerned, that nothing turn out badly," he said.

Menace reverberated in his voice, and it was evident that menace was something this individual dispensed daily. It was also clear that he need threaten but once, and in most instances, not even that. Even so, Alatriste twisted the tip of his mustache while he held his antagonist's gaze, frowning, and with his feet firmly planted, resolved not to be impressed by either an Excellency or a *sursum corda*. He did not like partial payments, and he liked even less to be lectured to at midnight by two strangers who hid their identity behind masks. But his less exacting companion with the pockmarked face seemed interested in other questions.

"What happens to their purses?" Alatriste heard him ask. "Must we deliver them as well?"

Italian, Alatriste decided when he heard the accent. The man spoke quietly and gravely, almost confidentially, but in a muffled, hoarse voice that was both disquieting and annoying. It was as if someone had poured raw alcohol over his vocal cords. His words were respectful, but a false note sounded through them—a kind of insolence that was no less disturbing for being veiled. He looked at the masked men with a smile that was at once friendly and sinister, a smile that was a flash of white beneath his trimly cut mustache. It was not difficult to imagine him with the same expression, as his knife—*rrriss, rrriss*—slit the clothing of a client, along with the flesh beneath it. It was a smile so oddly charming that it gave one cold chills.

"That will not be necessary," the round-headed man replied, after silently consulting his masked partner, who nodded. "You may keep the purses, if you wish. As a bonus."

The Italian quietly whistled an air, something like a chaconne, *ti-ri-tu, ta-ta*, repeated a couple of times, as he glanced at the captain out of the corner of his eye.

"I believe I am going to enjoy this job."

The smile disappeared from his lips, only to reappear in the black eyes, which glinted dangerously. That was the first time Alatriste saw Gualterio Malatesta smile, and the prelude to a long and troubled series of encounters. The captain would later tell me that at that very instant his thought was that if someone should smile at him like that in a lonely alleyway, he would not wait to see it twice, he would unsheathe his blade like lightning. To cross swords with that individual was to feel the urgent need to strike first, before he dealt a blow that was the last you would know. Picture, Your Mercies, a person by your side who is like a dangerous serpent, someone you can never be sure of, never certain which side he will take, until it is abundantly clear that he does not give a damn about either side, but only himself. One of those slippery, duplicitous, whichever-way-the-wind-blows types, with a bag of dirty tricks. A man with whom you could never lower your guard, and whom it behooves you to take out of the picture before he stabs you in the back.

Their portly soon-to-be-employer was a man of few words. Again he waited without speaking, listening attentively as the round-headed one explained to Diego Alatriste and the Italian the final details of their assignment. Twice the portly man nodded, signaling his approval of what he heard. Then he turned and walked toward the door.

"I do not want much blood," they heard him insist for the last time from the doorway.

From everything he had seen—the man's bearing, and especially the profound respect the second masked man showed him—the captain deduced that the person who had just left was of very high station. Alatriste was still thinking about that when the round-headed fellow rested one hand on the table and stared intently at him and the Italian. There was a new and disquieting gleam in his eyes, as if he still had not told them everything. An uncomfortable silence fell over the shadow-filled room, and Alatriste and the Italian kept glancing at each other, wordlessly wondering what was yet to come. Facing them, motionless, the masked man seemed to be waiting for something, or someone.

The answer came after a moment, when a tapestry, inconspicuous in the shadows between the bookshelves, moved to reveal a hidden door; in the opening they could see a dark and sinister silhouette, which someone less level-headed than Diego Alatriste might have taken for an apparition. The newcomer stepped forward and the table lamp illuminated his face, exaggerating hollows in his shaved sunken cheeks and the feverish light in a pair of eyes shadowed by thick eyebrows. He was wearing the black and white robes of the Dominicans, and he was not masked. His shining eyes lent an expression of fanaticism to the thin, ascetic face. He must have been close to fifty years old. His gray, tonsured hair was cut short like a helmet around his temples, and his hands, which he had taken from the sleeves of his robes when he entered, were dry and bony, like those of a cadaver. They looked as if they would be as icy as death.

The round-headed man turned toward the priest with extreme deference. "You heard everything, Reverend Father?"

The Dominican nodded briefly, never taking his eyes from Alatriste and the Italian, as though appraising them. Then he turned to the masked man and, as if that movement were a signal or an order, the latter again addressed the two hired swords.

"The caballero who just left us," he said, "is worthy of every respect and consideration. But it is not he alone who decides this affair, and it is best that we elaborate on a few details."

When he reached this point, the masked man exchanged a brief look with the priest, awaiting his approval before continuing. But the other remained impassive.

"For reasons originating at the highest level of government," the masked man then continued, "and despite what the caballero who has just left said, the two Englishmen must be removed from contention in a more . . ." He paused, as if seeking the appropriate words. ". . . in a more, hmm, *effective* manner." Again he glanced at the priest. "That is, more definitive."

"Do you, señor, wish to say . . ." began Diego Alatriste, who preferred to have things clear.

The Dominican, who had listened in silence and seemed to be growing impatient, interrupted, raising one of his bony hands.

"He 'wishes to say' that the two heretics must die."

"Both?"

"Both."

Beside Alatriste, the Italian again quietly whistled his little tune. *Ti-ri-tu, ta-ta.* His expression registered an emotion somewhere between interested and amused. The captain, slightly hesitant, looked at the money lying on the table. He thought a moment, then shrugged.

"No matter to me," he said. "And my companion seems not to object to the change in plans."

"I like it," the Italian said quickly, still smiling.

"It even makes things easier," Alatriste continued serenely. "At night it is more complicated to wound men than to dispatch them."

"The art of the simple," his companion added.

Now the captain looked at the masked man. "There is one thing that worries me," he said. "The caballero who just left seems to be a man of high caliber, and he said that he does not wish us to kill anyone. I do not know what my companion thinks, but I would prefer not to get on the wrong side of someone whom you yourself addressed as 'Excellency,' whoever he may be, in order to do Your Mercies' bidding."

"There could, perhaps, be more money," the masked one said, after a slight hesitation.

"It would be helpful to know exactly how much."

"Ten additional four-doubloon pieces. With the ten still to be paid, and these five, that will be twenty-five doubloons for each of you. Plus the purses of the most excellent Misters Thomas and John Smith."

"I am comfortable with that," said the Italian.

It was obvious that two or twenty made no difference to him: wounded, dead, or put up as pickles. As for Alatriste, he reflected again for a moment, then shook his head. That was a lot of doubloons for making sieves out of a pair of nobodies. And there, precisely, was the hitch in such a strange business: It was too well paid not to mean trouble. His instinct as a former soldier signaled danger.

"It isn't a question of money."

"There are swords to spare in Madrid," hinted the man with the mask, annoyed. The captain was not sure whether he meant in regard to looking for a substitute or for someone to settle scores if they refused the new arrangement. Alatriste was not pleased by the possibility that it was a threat. Out of habit, he twisted his mustache with his right hand as he slowly rested his left on the pommel of his sword. No one failed to register his move.

The priest whipped around to face Alatriste squarely. The ascetic's face had hardened, and his arrogant, sunken eyes bored into the captain's.

"I," he said in his disagreeable voice, "am Fray Emilio Bocanegra, president of the Holy Tribunal of the Inquisition."

With those words, an icy wind seemed to blow across the room. The priest made clear to Diego Alatriste and the Italian, succinctly, and menacingly, that he did not need a mask to hide his identity, or come to them like a thief in the night, because the power God had placed in his hands was sufficient to annihilate any enemy of the Holy Mother Church or His Catholic Majesty, the King of all the Spains. That said, while his listeners swallowed nervously, he paused to assess the effect of his words, then continued in the same threatening tone.

"Yours are sinful, mercenary hands, stained with blood like your swords and your consciences. But the Omnipotent Heavenly Father writes straight with crooked lines."

The crooked lines exchanged an uneasy glance as the priest continued. "Tonight," he said, "I am entrusting to you a task of sacred inspiration," and he added, "You are to fulfill it regardless of the cost, because in so doing you serve divine justice. If you refuse, if you cast aside the burden, the wrath of God will fall upon you through the long and terrible arm of the Holy Office. We are like muleteers. Ubiquitous and persistent."

With that the Dominican was silent, and no one dared speak a word. Even the Italian had forgotten his tra-la-las, and that said a lot.

In the Spain of that day, to quarrel with the powerful Inquisition meant to confront a series of horrors that often included prison, torture, the stake, and death. Even the toughest men trembled at the mention of the Holy Office, and for his part, Diego Alatriste, like all Madrid, knew very well the infamous reputation of Fray Emilio Bocanegra, president of the Council of Six Judges, whose influence reached as far as the Grand Inquisitor, and even the private corridors of the Royal Palace. Only a week before, because of a so-called *crimen pessimum*, Padre Bocanegra had convinced the tribunal to burn four young servants of the Conde de Monteprieto in the Plaza Mayor when, after being subjected to the Inquisitorial rack, they denounced each other as sodomites. As for the aristocratic count—himself a bachelor and a melancholy man—his title as a grandee of Spain had saved him from an identical fate by only a hair's breadth. The king contented himself with signing a decree to seize his possessions and send him into

exile in Italy. The merciless Bocanegra had personally con-
ducted the entire proceedings, and that triumph was the
last step in securing his fearsome power at court. Even the
Conde de Olivares, a favorite of the king, tried to please
the ferocious Dominican.

This was no time to so much as blink. Captain Alatriste
sighed deep inside, realizing that the two Englishmen,
whoever they might be and despite the good intentions of
the heavier masked man, had been sentenced without re-
prieve. They were dealing with the Church, and arguing
any further would be, in addition to fruitless, dangerous.

"What are we to do?" he said finally, resigned to the
inevitable.

"Kill them outright," Fray Emilio replied instantly, the
fire of fanaticism blazing in his eyes.

"Without knowing who they are?"

"We have already told you who they are," the masked
man with the round head reminded him. "Misters Thomas
and John Smith. English travelers."

"And ungodly Anglicans," added the priest, his voice
crackling with anger. "But you have no need to know who
they are. It is enough that they come from a land of
heretics—a treacherous people, anathema to Spain and the
Catholic religion. By executing God's will, you will render
a valuable service to the All Powerful and to the crown."

Having said this, the priest took out another purse containing twenty gold coins and disdainfully tossed it on the table.

"You see now," he added, "that divine justice, unlike the earthly kind, pays in advance, although over time it collects its return." He stared at the captain and the Italian as if engraving their faces in his memory. "No one escapes His eyes, and God knows very well where to come to collect His debts."

Diego Alatriste made as if to nod in agreement. He was a man with brass, but actually the gesture was an attempt to hide a shudder. The lamplight made the priest look diabolical, and the menace in his voice would have been enough to alter the composure of the bravest of men. Standing beside the captain, the Italian was pale, without his *ti-ri-tu, ta-ta* or his smile. Not even the round-headed man dared open his mouth.

III. A LITTLE LADY

Perhaps because a man's true homeland is his childhood, despite all the time that has gone by, I always remember the Tavern of the Turk with nostalgia. The place, Captain Alatriste, and those hazardous years of my boyhood are all gone now, but in the days of our Philip the Fourth, the tavern was one of four hundred in which the seventy thousand residents of Madrid could quench their thirst. That comes to about one tavern for every one hundred and seventy-five citizens. And that is not counting brothels, gaming houses, and other public establishments of, shall we say, relaxed or dubious moral ambience, which in a paradoxical, unique, and never-again-to-be-the-same Spain were visited as frequently as the churches—and often by the same people.

La Lebrijana's enterprise was in fact a cellar of the sort

where one came to eat, drink, and burn the night away, located on the corner of Calles Toledo and Arcabuz, about five hundred steps from the Plaza Mayor. The two rooms where Diego Alatriste and I lived were on the upper floor, and in a way the den below served as our sitting room. The captain liked to go down there to kill time when he had nothing better to do—which was often. Despite the smell of grease and smoke from the kitchen, the dirty floor and tables, and the mice running around, chased by the cat or looking for bread crumbs, it was a comfortable-enough place. It was also entertaining, because there were frequently travelers brought by post horse, and magistrates, tipstaves, flower vendors, and shopkeepers from the nearby Providencia and La Cebada plazas, as well as former soldiers drawn by the proximity of the principal streets of the city and the *mentidero* at San Felipe el Real, a center where idlers gathered to gossip. Not to disdain the tavern's attractions—a little faded but still splendid—and the longtime fame of the tavernkeeper and the Valdemoro wines—a muscatel as well as an aromatic San Martín de Valdeiglesias—but the place had another drawing card. It was blessed with a back gate that opened onto a courtyard and the next street, a very handy feature when one was slipping away from sheriffs, catchpoles, creditors, poets, friends in need of money, and other miscreants and inopportune guests.

As for Diego Alatriste, the table that Caridad la Lebrijana reserved for him near the door was commodious and sunny, and sometimes the wine brought with it a meat pie or some cracklings. The captain had carried over from his youth—something he said very little or nothing about—a certain taste for reading. It was not unusual to see him sitting at his table, alone, his sword and hat hung on a peg in the wall, reading the printed version of Lope's latest play—he was the captain's favorite author—recently performed in El Príncipe or La Cruz. Or it might be one of the gazettes or broadsides featuring the anonymous satiric verses that circulated at court in that time that was at once magnificent, decadent, mournful, and inspired—a time that cast a shadow as black as a curate's cloak over the favorite, the monarchy, and the morning star. In many verses, in fact, Alatriste recognized the corrosive wit and proverbial bad temper of his friend the unredeemed grumbler and popular poet don Francisco de Quevedo:

> *Here lies Señor Pérez, the swine*
> *Whose life was Satan's appetizer*
> *While his devil's broth was stewing.*
> *No pussy ever meowed to him.*
> *How he rued Herod's misconstruing*
> *The use of power; so much wiser*
> *Not to have slaughtered innocent lambs:*

Forsooth! Such succulent cherubim
Should be spared and saved for screwing.

And other pretty bits of the sort. I imagine that my poor widowed mother, back there in her tiny Basque town, would have been alarmed had she had a hint of what strange company my serving as the captain's page had led me into. But as for the young Íñigo Balboa, at thirteen he found that world to be a fascinating spectacle, and a singular school of life.

I mentioned a couple of chapters ago that don Francisco, along with Licenciado Calzas, Juan Vicuña, Dómine Pérez, the pharmacist Fadrique, and others of the captain's friends, often came to the tavern, and engaged in long discussions about politics, theater, poetry, and routinely, a punctilious appraisal of the many wars in which our poor Spain had been or was then involved. She may still have been powerful and feared by other nations, but she was touched with death in her soul. The battlefields of those wars were skillfully re-created on the tavern table by Juan Vicuña, using bits of bread, cutlery, and jugs of wine. Originally from Extremadura, and badly wounded at Nieuwpoort, he had once been a sergeant in the horse guard, and deemed himself a master strategist.

War had soon become a real and pressing concern, for it was during the affair of the masked men and the

Englishmen, as I recall, that hostilities were renewed in the Low Countries, after the expiration of the twelve-year truce that our deceased and peaceful King Philip the Third, the father of our young monarch, had signed with the Low Dutch. That long interim of peace, or its effects, was precisely the reason so many veteran soldiers were wandering without employ through the Spains and the rest of the world, swelling the ranks of idle braggarts, bullies, and blusterers disposed to hire out for any petty villainy. And among them we may count Diego Alatriste. However, the captain was one of the silent variety, and in contrast to so many others, no one ever saw him boasting of his campaigns or his wounds. And then when the drumrolls of his old company sounded again, Alatriste, like my father and many other brave men, rushed to reenlist beneath the old general of their old *tercio*, don Ambrosio de Spínola, and to play their part at the beginning of what today we know as the Thirty Years' War. He would have served on and on had he not received the serious wound at Fleurus.

At any rate, although the war against Holland and in the rest of Europe was the topic of conversation those days, I rarely heard the captain refer to his life as a soldier. That made me admire him even more, accustomed as I was to crossing paths with a hundred swaggering braggarts who, talking out of both sides of their mouth and fantasizing about Flanders, spent the day trumpeting their supposed feats at full pitch, clanking their swords through the Puerta del Sol or along Calle Montera, and strutting like peacocks on the steps of San Felipe. Their sashes were stuffed with tin tubes filled with documents praising their campaigns and their bravery, all of them ringing falser than a lead doubloon.

It had rained a little, early that morning, and there were muddy tracks on the tavern floor, and that smell of dampness and sawdust that public places get on rainy days. The clouds were breaking, and a ray of sun, timid at first but soon after very sure of itself, framed the table where Diego Alatriste, Licenciado Calzas, Dómine Pérez, and Juan Vicuña were chatting after a meal. I was sitting on a taboret near the door, practicing my penmanship with a quill, an inkwell, and a ream of paper the *licenciado* had brought me at the captain's suggestion. "So he will be able to instruct himself and read law and bleed the last *maravedís* out of clients, like all you lawyers, scribes, and other bloodsucking varlets."

Calzas had burst out laughing. He was a pleasant fellow with a kind of cynical good humor, and his friendship with Alatriste was old and trusting.

"My faith! What a great truth that is," he had replied,

still amused, and winking at me. "The pen, Íñigo, is a better source of income than the sword."

"*Longa manus calami*," the good father put it.

A principle about which all those gathered around the table were in agreement, either in cordial accord or to hide that they did not know Latin. The next day the *licenciado* brought me a gift of writing materials, which no doubt he had skillfully extracted from the courts, where, thanks to the corrupt practices of his office, he earned an easy livelihood. Alatriste said nothing, and he did not offer me counsel on what use to make of the pen, paper, and ink. But I read the approval in his calm eyes when he saw me sitting beside the door practicing my letters. I did that by copying a few of Lope's verses I had sometimes heard the captain recite on nights when the Fleurus wound tormented him more than usual.

> *The bastard has not come, as planned,*
> *Whose design it was on this fair day*
> *To die by my genteel and noble hand*
> *And, in so doing, gain cachet.*

The fact that the captain would occasionally laugh quietly as he recited those lines, perhaps to gloss over the pain of his old wound, was not enough to cloud the fact that I longed for pretty verses. Like others I applied myself to copying that morning, having heard them also during the captain's long, sleepless nights.

Hand to hand I must duel with him
Where all Seville may see,
In the plaza or in the lane;
For he who kills with treachery
Will ne'er outlive the shame,
And he whose blood is vilely spilled
Gains more than him by whom he's killed.

I had just finished writing the last line when the captain, who had gotten up to get a drink from the water jug, took my paper to look it over. Standing beside me, he read the verses to himself and then fixed his eyes on me: one of those gazes I knew so well, serene and prolonged, as eloquent as the words I grew used to reading on his lips though they were never voiced. I remember that the sun, still an I-want-to-but-I-can't between the roof tiles of Calle Toledo, aimed an oblique ray at the rest of the pages in my lap, as well as the captain's gray-green, almost transparent eyes, and dried the last of the fresh ink of the verses Diego Alatriste held in his hand. He did not smile, or make a single gesture. Without a word he handed me the sheet of paper and went back to the table, but from there he sent me a last long look before again joining in conversation with his friends.

Then, only a brief interval apart, came El Tuerto Fadrique, his one eye a little red, and don Francisco de Quevedo. Fadrique had come straight from his apothecary shop at the Puerta Cerrada; he had been preparing specifics for ailing clients, and his gullet was burning from the effects of vapors, elixirs, and medicinal powders. Thus the minute he walked in the door, he wrapped an arm around a large bottle of Valdemoro wine and began to detail to Dómine Pérez the laxative properties of the hull of a black nut from Hindustan. That was the scene when don Francisco de Quevedo stepped inside, scraping the mud from his shoes.

"The mud that serves me, counsels me. . . ."

He was reciting as he entered, and clearly feeling fractious. He stopped at my side, adjusted his spectacles, glanced over the verses I was copying down, and raised his eyebrows, pleased to find that they were not lines from Alarcón or Góngora. Then he limped over to the table, with that gait demanded by his twisted feet—he had hobbled since he was a boy, something that had not gotten in the way of his being an agile and skillful swordsman—to sit down with the rest of his companions. And there he grabbed the closest jug.

"Share. Be not miserly with me,
But pour divine Bacchus's bounty...."

He directed this appeal toward Juan Vicuña. As I have said, Vicuña, who was very strong and brawny, had been a sergeant in the horse guard, had lost his right arm at Nieuwpoort, and now lived on his pension, which consisted of a license to run a small gaming house. Vicuña passed him a jug of Valdemoro, and although don Francisco preferred the white from Valdeiglesias, he emptied it without taking a breath.

"What news of your petition?" Vicuña asked with interest.

The poet swiped his mouth with the back of his hand. A few drops of wine had fallen on the cross of Santiago embroidered on the breast of his black sleeved doublet.

"I believe," he said, "that Philip the Great is wiping his ass with it."

"That itself is an honor," Licenciado Calzas argued.

Don Francisco appropriated another jug.

"In that case"—there was a pause as he drank—"the honor is to his royal ass. The paper was good, a half-ducat a ream. And I wrote it in my best hand."

He was in a foul mood, for these were not good times for him, not for his prose or his poetry, or his finances. Only a few weeks earlier, the fourth Philip had had to lift the decree—first prison and then exile—that had been weighing over Quevedo since the fall from favor, two or three years before, of his friend and protector the Duque de Osuna. At last reinstated, don Francisco had been able to return to Madrid, but he was in a monetary fast. His petition to the king, soliciting his former pension of four hundred *escudos* owed for service in Italy—he had been a spy in Venice, a fugitive, and two of his companions had been executed—had been answered with silence. That had made him more furious than ever, and his fury nourished his bad humor and his wit, which went hand in hand . . . and contributed to new problems.

"*Patientia lenietur princeps,*" Dómine Pérez said, consoling him. "Patience placates the sovereign."

"Well, Reverend Father, it does not placate me one whit."

The Jesuit looked around with a preoccupied air. Every time one of this group found himself in difficulty, it fell to the *dómine* to speak to his character and his conduct, as befitted his position as man of the Church. From time to time, he absolved his friends *sub conditione*, without their requesting it. Behind their backs, the captain said. Less devious than the norm among members of his order, the *dómine* took seriously the honored obligation to moderate squabbles. He was full of life, a good theologian, tolerant of human weaknesses, benevolent, and placid in the extreme. He made generous allowances for his fellow beings, and his church was crowded with women who came to confess their sins, drawn by his reputation for being generous at the tribunal of penitence.

As for the regulars at the Tavern of the Turk, in his presence no one spoke of dark deeds or of women; that was the condition upon which his company was based: tolerance, and friendship. Quarrels and affairs, he often said, I will deal with in the confessional. And when his ecclesiastical superiors reproached him for passing time in the tavern with poets and swordsmen, he responded that saints save themselves, while sinners must be sought out. I will add on his behalf that he barely tasted his wine and I never heard him speak ill of anyone. Which in the Spain of that day—and today as well—was something unheard of in a cleric.

"Let us be prudent, Señor Quevedo," he added affectionately that day, after his comment in Latin. "You, sir, are not in a position to speak ill of certain things aloud."

Don Francisco looked at the priest, adjusting his eyeglasses. "I? Speak ill? You err, Dómine. I do not speak ill, I merely state the truth."

And then he stood, and turned toward the rest of those in the tavern, reciting, in his educated, sonorous, and clear voice:

"I shall speak out, despite appeals.
You touch first your lips, and then your brow
Counseling silence or threatening fear.
Should not a man hold courage dear?
Must he not feel the thing he says?
Must he not say the thing he feels?"

Juan Vicuña and Licenciado Calzas applauded, and El Tuerto Fadrique nodded gravely. Captain Alatriste looked at don Francisco with a broad, melancholy smile, which the poet returned. Dómine Pérez, acknowledging that the question the poet had posed was unanswerable, concentrated on his watered muscatel. The poet took up the charge again, now approaching it via a sonnet that he kept revising.

"I looked upon the walls of my fatherland,
Though once strong, now tumbling down. . . ."

Caridad la Lebrijana came and took away the empty jars, asking for moderation before swishing away with a walk that captured all eyes except those of the *dómine*, still absorbed in his muscatel, and of don Francisco, sunk in combat with silent ghosts.

"I walked into my home and saw
A ruin that nothing could assuage;

My staff, more curved and battered.
My sword, now dulled by age,
In all a memory of death:
Nothing was left . . .

   nothing that mattered."

Some strangers strolled into the tavern, and Diego Alatriste placed a hand on the poet's arm, calming him. "The memory of death!" don Francisco repeated in conclusion, lost in his own thoughts. He sat, however, and accepted the new jar the captain offered him.

In truth, Señor Quevedo's days at court were spent with orders of arrest or exile hanging over his head. Although occasionally he bought a house whose administrator milked him of the rents, that may have been the reason he had never wanted a fixed residence in Madrid, and tended to take lodgings in public inns. Truces from his adversaries, like periods of prosperity, were brief for this singular man, the hobgoblin of his enemies and delight of his friends, who one moment might be mingling with nobles and scholars and the next scrabbling in his purse for the last *maravedí*. Changes of fortune . . . which so loves to change, and almost never for the better.

"We have no choice but to fight," the poet added after a few seconds.

His tone was pensive, as if for himself only; one eye was

swimming in wine, and the other had gone down for the last time. Alatriste, still holding his friend's arm and bending over the table, smiled with affectionate sadness.

"Against whom, don Francisco?"

The captain seemed almost not to expect an answer. Quevedo raised one finger. His eyeglasses had slipped from his nose and were dangling from their cord, nearly dipping into his wine.

"Against stupidity, evil, superstition, envy, and ignorance," he enunciated slowly, and as he spoke, he appeared to regard his reflection on the surface of the liquid. "Which is to say, against all Spain. Against everything."

I was listening from where I was sitting by the door, intrigued and uneasy. I intuited that behind don Francisco's bad-humored words lay dark reasons that he himself could not comprehend, but that went beyond simple tantrums and sour character. I, at my tender age, still did not know that it is possible to speak harshly about what we love, precisely because of that love, and with the moral authority that love bestows upon us. Later, I was able to understand that the state of affairs in Spain was very painful to don Francisco. A Spain still formidable from without, but one that despite the pomp and artifice, despite our young and charming king, our national pride and our heroic battles,

Spain had begun to doze, trusting in the gold and silver that the galleons brought from the Indies. But all that gold and silver disappeared into the hands of the aristocracy, and of lazy, corrupt, and unproductive officials and clergy who squandered it in vain undertakings such as financing the costly war renewed in Flanders, where providing a pike, that is, a new pikeman or soldier, cost an eye and a leg.

Even the Low Dutch whom we were fighting sold us their manufactured products and made commercial deals right in Cádiz, acquiring the precious metals that our ships—which had to outmaneuver pirates—brought from the lands to the west. Aragonese and Catalans were shielded by their laws; Portugal was patched together; commerce was in the hands of foreigners; finances were the purview of Genoese bankers; and no one worked except the wretched peasants, exploited by the tax collectors of the aristocracy and the king. And in the midst of all that corruption and madness, moving against the course of history, like a beautiful, terrifying animal that still slashed and clawed yet at the heart was eaten by a malignant tumor, our poor Spain was worm-eaten inside, condemned to an inexorable decadence that did not escape the clear eyes of don Francisco de Quevedo. But I, at that time, could see nothing but the daring of his words, and I kept looking anxiously outside, expecting at any moment to see the catchpoles of the *corregidor* appear with a new warrant for don Francisco's arrest, to punish his arrogant lack of caution.

That was when I saw the carriage. It would be shading the truth to deny that I was waiting for it to pass, for it drove up Calle Toledo two or three times a week, more or less at the same hour. It was black, lined with leather and red velvet, and the coachman was not in the coach box driving the mules but, rather, rode one of them—the normal procedure for that kind of carriage. The coach itself was solid but discreet, typical of owners who enjoyed a good position but had no right, or inclination, to parade their wealth. Someone like a rich merchant or a high official who, while not privileged nobility, held a powerful post at court.

As for me, I was interested only in the contents, not the container. In that still-childlike hand, white as rice paper, that was just visible, resting discreetly on the frame of the small window. In that golden gleam of long, blond curls. And in those eyes. Despite the years that have passed since I first saw those eyes, and the many adventures and troubles those blue irises would bring to my life in the years that followed, still today I am incapable of expressing in writing the effect of that bright, pure gaze . . . so deceptively limpid, and of a color identical to the Madrid skies that don Diego Velázquez, later the favorite painter of our lord and king, learned to paint like no other.

At the time of my story, Angélica de Alquézar must have been around eleven or twelve years old, and she was already a promise of the splendid beauty she would become, beauty of which Velázquez himself would give a good account in the famous portrait she posed for sometime around 1635. But more than a decade earlier, on those March mornings just before the adventure of the Englishmen, I did not know who the youthful, almost childish girl was who every two or three days rode in her carriage up Calle Toledo toward the Plaza Mayor and the Alcázar Real, where—I later learned—she attended the queen and young princesses as a *menina*, a lady-in-waiting. That privilege was due largely to the position of her uncle from Aragon, Luis de Alquézar, at the time one of the king's most influential secretaries. To me, the young blonde girl in the carriage was simply a celestial, wondrous vision; she was as far removed from my poor mortal condition as the sun or the most beautiful star is from this corner on Calle Toledo, where the wheels of her carriage and the hooves of the mules arrogantly spattered anyone in their path.

That morning, however, something altered the routine. Instead of passing the tavern and continuing up the street, allowing me the usual fleeting vision of its blonde passenger, the carriage stopped just before it reached me, some twenty steps from the Tavern of the Turk. The mud had pasted a large sliver from a barrel stave onto one of the spokes, and it had worked its way into the axle, jamming the wheel. The coachman had no choice but to stop the mules and slip down to the ground, or mud, to be exact, to free the wheel. It happened that the group of boys who were always hanging about on that corner gathered closer to jeer at the coachman, and he, annoyed, took up his whip to run them off. He never accomplished it. The street urchins of Madrid then were as pesky and persistent as a swarm of bot flies—*In any quarrel, the one born in Madrid wins the laurel*, goes an old saying—and besides, it was not every day that they were offered a diversion like a carriage on which to practice their aim. And so, armed with clumps of mud, they began to exhibit a skill with their projectiles that the most experienced harque-busier would have envied.

I jumped up, alarmed. The fate of the coachman was of no consequence to me, but the carriage was transporting something that at that stage in my young life was the most precious cargo imaginable. Besides, was I not the son of Lope Balboa, a man who died gloriously in the wars of our lord and king? So I had no choice. Resolved to do battle immediately for someone I considered my lady—always from afar and with the greatest respect—I charged the young hellions, and with two blows of my fists and four stout kicks sent the enemy forces flying, leaving me champion of the field.

The direction of my attack—in line with my secret desire, it must be told—had brought me close to the carriage. The coachman was not a grateful type, so after giving me a surly look, he returned to his work. I was just about to leave, when those blue eyes appeared at the window. The vision froze me where I stood, and I felt blood rush to my face with the speed of a musket ball. The girl, the young lady, focused on me with an intensity that could have stopped the flow of water in the nearby fountain. Blonde. Pale. Painfully beautiful. Why I am telling you this? She did not even smile, she merely stared at me with curiosity. It was obvious that my gesture had not gone unnoticed. As for me, that look, that apparition, more than compensated for my trouble. I lifted my hand to an imaginary hat and bowed.

"Íñigo Balboa, at your s-service," I stammered, although managing to give my words a certain firmness I judged to be gallant. "Page in the service of Captain don Diego Alatriste."

The girl held my gaze, never changing expression. The coachman had climbed onto his mule and slapped the reins, and the carriage began to roll. I took one step back to avoid being spattered by the wheels, and at that instant she again placed a small, perfect, white-as-mother-of-pearl hand on the edge of the window frame, and I felt as if I had been given it to kiss. Then the corners of her mouth, perfectly sketched on pale lips, lifted slightly, nothing more than a flicker that could be interpreted as a distant, enigmatic, and mysterious smile. I heard the coachman's whip crack, and the carriage jerked away, carrying with it that smile which I still today cannot swear was real or imagined. And I was left standing in the middle of the street, enslaved by love, watching that girl who to me was a blonde angel. Poor fool that I was, oblivious of the fact that I had just met my sweetest, most dangerous, and mortal enemy.

IV. THE AMBUSH

In March it grew dark early. There were streaks of light in the sky, but beneath the eaves of the roof tiles the streets were black as a wolf's mouth. Captain Alatriste and his companion had chosen a narrow, lonely lane that the two Englishmen would have to follow on the way to the House of Seven Chimneys. A messenger had advised them of the hour and the route. He had also brought the most recent description of their victims, to prevent error. Mister Thomas Smith, the blonder and older of the two, was riding a dapple-gray horse and wearing a gray travel suit with discreet silver adornments, high boots also dyed gray, and a hat with a band of the same color. As for Mister John Smith, the younger man, he was riding a bay. His suit was chestnut brown, his boots saddle-colored, and his hat sported three small white plumes. After several days of riding, both were looking dusty and fatigued. They had little luggage: two portmanteaus strapped onto the croups of their mounts.

Hidden in the shadow of an arched entry, Diego Alatriste looked toward the lantern that he and his companion had placed at a bend in the street so that it would throw light on the travelers before they could see their attackers. The lane, which turned at a sharp right angle, began at Calle Barquillo, near the palace of the Conde de Guadalmedina and, after skimming the orchard wall of the Discalced Carmelite convent, ended at the House of Seven Chimneys, near the crossing of Calle Torres and Las Infantas. The place chosen for the ambush was in the first section, which had the darkest and tightest turn, where two horsemen taken by surprise could easily be overcome.

It grew a little cooler, and the captain wrapped himself more tightly in his new cape, bought with the advance, in gold, from the masked men. As he moved, the clink of metal was audible: the *vizcaína* ticked the hilt of the sword and the grip of the loaded and well-oiled pistol thrust in the back of his belt. It might be necessary, in the worst case, to resort to such a noisy and definitive expedient, something expressly forbidden for pragmatic reasons but in difficult situations an opportune solution. That night, Alatriste had rounded out his attire with a buffalo-hide jerkin that would protect his body from an antagonist's knife, and his own slaughterer's blade hidden in the leg of one of his old boots, the ones with comfortable and well-worn soles that would give him good footing once the dance began.

> *"Oh unlucky the madman*
> *Who unbuckles his sword . . ."*

Alatriste began to recite to himself, to make the time pass. He murmured a few more fragments from Lope de Vega's *The Sheep Well*, one of his favorite dramas, before he again fell silent, his face hidden beneath the wide brim of his hat, which he had pulled down to his eyebrows.

Another shadow moved slightly, a few steps from where he was standing beneath the arch of the gate that led to the garden of the Carmelite priests. After a long half-hour of immobility, the Italian must have been as cold and stiff as the captain was. The Italian was a strange one. He had come to the rendezvous dressed in black, wrapped in his black cape and wearing a black hat, and his pockmarked face had brightened with a smile only when Alatriste suggested they set the lantern where it would light the bend of the lane they had chosen for the ambush.

"I like that," was all the Italian said, in that choked, harsh voice. "They will be in the light and we in the shadow. Seen and unseen."

Then he had whistled the little phrase he seemed so fond of, *ti-ri-tu, ta-ta*, while in an expeditious, professional tone they planned the assault. Alatriste would take on the older of the two men, the gray-suited Englishman riding the dapple-gray, while the Italian would dispatch the man in brown riding the bay. No pistol shots, if possible, for everything should happen with enough stealth that when the job was done they could search the luggage, find the documents, and, of course, relieve the cold meat of the money they were carrying. If there was an uproar that attracted witnesses, it would blow the whole plan to hell. In addition, the House of Seven Chimneys was not far away, and the servants of the English ambassador might come to the aid of their compatriots. What was needed, therefore, was a quick and deadly operation: *cling, clang*; greetings and godspeed. And their English starlings would be halfway to Hell, or wherever Anglican heretics ended up. At least those two were not going to yell at the top of their lungs for confession, as good Catholics did, waking half of Madrid.

The captain settled his cape more comfortably and looked toward the bend of the lane lighted by the wan glow of the lantern. Beneath the warm cloak, his left hand rested on the pommel of his sword. For a while he entertained himself by trying to remember the number of men he had killed—not in war, where in the midst of battle it was impossible to know the result of a sword thrust or ball from a harquebus—but, rather, up close. Face to face. The matter of the face was important, or at least it was to Diego Alatriste; unlike other hired bravos, he had never knifed a man in the back. True, he did not always allow much time for his victim to assume an ideal stance, but it is also true that he never made a move toward anyone who was not facing him with his weapon unsheathed—except for one Hollandish sentinel whose neck he slit at night. But that was war, which was also the case of certain Germans who had mutinied in Maastricht, and all the other opponents killed during campaigns. None of this meant a great deal according to the standards of the time, but the captain was a man who needed something that would enable him to preserve at least a shred of self-respect. On the chessboard of life, every man makes what moves he can, and however feeble his alibi may be, it is a kind of justification. And though it might not be sufficient—as could be seen in his eyes when liquor floated up the devils that tied his soul in knots—it did, at least, give him something to cling to when the nausea was so intense that he caught himself staring down the round black barrel of a pistol.

Eleven, he concluded. Without counting the wars. Four in duels with Flemish and Italian soldiers, then another in Madrid, and another in Seville. All over gambling, angry words, or women. The rest had been for pay: five lives at so much per death. All strong, sturdy men capable of defending themselves, and a few of them ruffians of ill repute. No remorse, except in two cases: one—a certain lady's lover whose cuckolded husband did not have the backbone to saw off his cuckold's horns himself—had drunk too much the night that Diego Alatriste stepped out before him in a badly lighted street. The captain never forgot his stunned look, his inability to comprehend what was happening, and by the time his victim had drawn a trembling sword from its sheath, he found himself with a handspan of steel in his chest. The other had been a pretty-boy at court, a conceited youth always beribboned and beflounced, whose very existence was a thorn in the side of the Conde de Guadalmedina because of certain lawsuits, wills, and inheritances. So the count had engaged Diego Alatriste to simplify the legal tangles. Everything was resolved during young Marqués Álvaro de Soto's outing with some friends to the Acero fountain to flirt with the ladies who came to take the waters on the far side of the Segovia bridge. Some pretext: a push, a couple of exchanged insults, and the youth, barely twenty, cursing the whoreson who had bumped him, slapped a fatal hand to his sword. Everything happened in a flash, and before anyone could react, Captain Alatriste and the two men who covered his back had vanished, leaving young Álvaro de Soto flat on his back and bleeding to death before the horrified eyes of the ladies and their attendants. That matter caused a bit of a stir, but Guadalmedina's influence provided protection for his hired swordsman. Nonetheless uncomfortable, Alatriste took with him the memory of the anguish in the face of the young man, who hadn't the slightest desire to fight this stranger with the fierce mustache, pale, cold eyes, and threatening mien, but was forced to put hand to steel because his friends and the ladies were watching. Without preamble, the captain had pierced the youth's throat with a simple circular thrust while he was still struggling to strike an airy stance—en garde: torso erect and face composed—trying desperately to remember the elegant moves his fencing master had taught him.

Eleven, Alatriste remembered. And except for the young marquis and one of the Flemish duelers, a soldier named Carmelo Tejada, he could not remember their names. Or perhaps he had never known them. At any rate, there in the shadows of the archway, waiting for the victims of the ambush, with the pain of that still-recent wound that kept him anchored in the capital, Diego Alatriste longed for the fields of Flanders, the *crack!* of the harquebuses and the neighing of horses, the sweat of combat alongside his comrades, the beat of drums, and the tranquil pace of men marching onto the battlefield, old flags flying. Rather than Madrid, and that lane where he was prepared to kill two men he had never seen in his life, what he longed for was a clear, faraway night when the enemy was the man you found before you, and God—it was said—was always on your side.

The clock in the Carmelite tower struck eight. And only shortly after, as if the bells of the church had been a signal, the sound of horses' hooves echoed down the lane from around the corner formed by the convent wall. Diego Alatriste looked toward the other shadow huddled in the archway, and a whistled tune indicated that his companion, too, was alert. The captain untied the cord at the neck of his cape, slid out of it so it would not hinder his movements, then rolled it up and left it in the archway. His eyes never left the corner lighted by the lantern as the sound of shod horses slowly came nearer. From the Italian's hiding place, yellowish light glinted off bare steel.

The captain adjusted his buffcoat and drew his sword from its scabbard. Now the sound of hooves came from the very bend in the lane, and a first, disproportionally large, shadow fell on the wall and moved along it. Alatriste took five or six deep breaths to empty the bad humors from his chest and, feeling lucid and in good form, stepped from the shelter of the archway, sword in his right hand as with his left he drew the *vizcaína*. As he emerged from the darkness of the entryway, another shadow moved forward, metal gleaming in both hands, and alongside the captain's, slipped down the lane toward the two human forms the lantern was throwing against the wall. One step, two, another. Everything was devilishly tight in the narrow alleyway, and as the shadows turned the corner they merged into a great jumble: burnished steel, startled eyes, the rough breathing of the Italian as he chose his victim and rushed toward him. The two travelers were walking their horses, reins in hand, and at first everything was very easy, except for the instant when Alatriste looked from one to the other, trying to identify his target. His Italian companion was quicker, or was improvising, for the captain heard him rush like an exhalation toward the closer of the candidates, perhaps because he had recognized his prey, or perhaps because, ignoring their earlier agreement, he had simply chosen the one in the lead, who had less time to react. Alatriste could see a young blond man in a chestnut-brown suit holding the reins of a bay horse; the young man cried out with alarm as he jumped aside to avoid, miraculously, the knife the Italian had aimed at him.

"Steenie! Steenie!"

It seemed more a shout to alert his companion than a call for help. Alatriste heard the Englishman yell twice as he ran past him. Skirting the horse—which, feeling itself free of the reins, was rearing and striking out with its forelegs—the captain raised his sword toward the other

Englishman, the one dressed in gray. By the light of the lantern, Alatriste could see that he was extraordinarily handsome, with very blond hair and a fine mustache. This second youth had just dropped the reins of his mount, and as he stepped back he drew his sword with the speed of lightning. Heretic or good Christian, that placed things in the proper perspective, so as the Englishman, some distance away, positioned his sword to defend himself, Alatriste planted one foot, stepped forward on the other, and engaged his opponent. As soon as he freed his sword, Alatriste made a lateral slash with the *vizcaína* to ward off the next thrust and rattle his opponent. An instant later, the younger man had been driven back four paces and was desperately defending himself, back against the wall, with no room to maneuver. The captain, methodically and confidently, prepared to thrust three-quarters of his blade through the first available opening and finish things off. Which was as good as done, for although the youth fought skillfully and valiantly, he was too fiery and too wild: he was defeating himself. Through his concentration, Alatriste heard the clash of the Italian's and the other Englishman's swords, their heavy breathing, and their curses. Out of the corner of his eye he caught a glimpse of their shadows on the wall.

Then, along with the clatter of the swords, the captain

heard a moan, and saw the shadow of the younger
Englishman slip down the wall. He seemed to be wounded,
defending himself, on one knee, with greater and greater
difficulty. That distracted Alatriste's adversary, and he
abandoned his instinct for survival and the skill with
which, up to that moment, he had defended himself.

Parrying a thrust, he shouted, "Mercy for my friend,"
in an elementary, strongly accented Spanish. And again,
"Mercy for my friend!"

He had dropped his guard slightly, and at his first care-
less instant, the captain, after a feint with the dagger, easily disarmed him. *Pardiez*, the heretic's balls are hung
right, he thought. What the devil was this business of asking for mercy for the other man when he himself was
about to give up the ghost? The foreigner's sword was still
flying through the air when Alatriste pressed the tip of his
own to the young man's throat, and drew back his elbow
slightly, which he needed to do in order to obtain the best
line for his thrust. Do away with him once and for all.
Mercy for my friend, indeed. The man had to be a bit dim,
or English, to shout something like that in a dark lane in
Madrid, with swords flashing all around him.

Then the Englishman repeated his strange behavior.
Instead of asking for mercy for himself—it was clear that
he was brave—or trying to pull out the useless poniard

still at his waist, he threw a desperate look toward his companion, who was weakly defending himself on one knee, and again cried to Diego Alatriste, "Mercy for my friend!"

The captain held up for a moment, bewildered. This blond youth with the carefully tended mustache, long hair—tousled, it was true, from travel—his elegant gray suit covered with dust, feared only for his friend, who was at the point of being dispatched by the Italian. Only at that moment, in the light of the lantern faithfully illuminating the scene of combat, did Alatriste allow himself to truly look at the Englishman: blue eyes; pale, finely modeled face contorted by anguish that was palpably not fear of losing his own life. Soft white hands. All marks of an aristocrat. Everything shouted breeding. And that, the captain told himself quickly, as he reviewed his conversation with the masked men—the wish of one not to have much blood, and the insistence of the other, backed by the Inquisitor Bocanegra, to murder the travelers—began to light too many dark corners for him to do away with this man and still live in peace.

So shit. A shithouse of shit. God damn him! *And* all the powers of night and devils of Hell! Still with his sword pressed to the Englishman's throat, Diego Alatriste hesitated, and his victim realized he was hesitating. Then, with a gesture of supreme nobility, incredible in his situation, he looked into Alatriste's eyes and slowly placed his hand on his breast, over his heart, as if he were making a solemn oath, not a plea.

"Mercy."

He asked for the last time, almost confidentially, in a low voice. And Diego Alatriste, who was still calling on all the demons, knew that now he could not kill the accursed Englishman in cold blood, at least not that night, in that place. And he also knew, as he lowered his sword and turned toward the Italian and the other youth, that he was on the verge, complete imbecile that he was, of walking into yet one more trap in his eventful life.

It was clear that the Italian was doing very well. He could have killed the wounded man any number of times, but he was satisfied to harass him with false lunges and feints, as though he were enjoying delaying the thrust home. He resembled a thin black cat toying with a mouse before sinking its claws into it. At his feet, knee on the ground and back against the wall, one hand clutching the wound bleeding through his clothing, the younger Englishman was trying not to faint, and barely parrying his adversary's attacks. He did not ask for mercy; instead, his face, mortally pallid, showed dignified determination; his teeth were clenched, and he was resolved to die without crying out or moaning.

"Leave off!" Alatriste shouted to the Italian. Between

thrusts, the captain's cohort looked at him, surprised to see him beside the second Englishman, who was disarmed and still standing. The attacker hesitated an instant, looked back at his subjected opponent, made a halfhearted feint, and again looked toward the captain.

"Is that a jest?" he asked, stepping back to catch his breath, as he whipped his sword through the air, right and left.

"Leave off," Alatriste insisted.

The Italian stared at him open-mouthed, unable to believe what he had just heard. In the dying light of the lantern, his pockmarked face looked like the surface of the moon. His black mustache twisted into a sinister smile, revealing his gleaming white teeth.

"Don't fuck this up now," the Italian said finally.

Alatriste took one step toward him, and the Italian looked at the sword in his hand. On his knee, uncomprehending, the wounded youth shifted his eyes from one to the other.

"There is more to this than we thought," the captain stated. "So we will kill them another day."

The Italian stared even harder. His smile grew wider and more incredulous, and then disappeared. He shook his head.

"You are mad," he said. "This could cost us our necks."

"I will take the responsibility."

"So?"

The Italian seemed to be thinking it over. Then, with the speed of a comet, he lunged at the Englishman with a thrust so forceful that had Alatriste not blocked his sword it would have pinned the youth to the wall. Stymied, the black-clad figure whirled toward the captain with an oath, and this time it was Alatriste who had to call on his instincts as a swordsman to fend off a second thrust, which came within a hair of the site of his heart. The Italian had attacked with the most vicious intentions in the world.

"We will meet again!" he cried. "Somewhere."

And kicking over the lantern as he ran, the Italian disappeared into the darkness of the street, again a shadow among shadows. From far away, his laugh echoed for an instant, like the worst of auguries.

V. THE TWO ENGLISHMEN

The younger man was not seriously wounded. His companion and Diego Alatriste had carried him closer to the lantern, which they lighted again. There they propped him against the Carmelites' garden wall and examined the knife wound he had received. It was a superficial cut that bled freely but was of no great consequence, the much-favored kind that allowed young dandies to strut before the ladies with an arm in a sling, at very little cost.

The man in the gray suit placed a clean handkerchief over the wound, which was beneath the left armpit, and then buttoned his friend's shirt and doublet, all the while speaking softly in their own tongue. During this procedure, which the Englishman performed with his back turned to Alatriste, as if he no longer feared anything from him, the captain had the opportunity to mull over certain interesting details. For example: Belying the apparent calm of the youth in gray, his hands were trembling as he opened his companion's clothing to ascertain the gravity of the wound. Also, although the captain knew only a few words of English, those shouted from one ship to another or from parapet to parapet in battle—a veteran soldier's vocabulary, limited to *Fock you, sunsa beechez,* and *We gon eslice off yu balls*—the captain could hear that the gray-clad man addressed his companion with a kind of affectionate respect. Further, though the injured man had called him Steenie, which was undoubtedly a friendly and familiar name or nickname, the latter used the formal "Milord" when speaking to the younger man. There was a cat in the creamery, here, but not exactly an alley cat: a purebred Angora.

All these things piqued Alatriste's curiosity, enough that instead of making himself scarce, as his common sense was screaming at him to do, he stood there quietly beside the two Englishmen whom he had been on the verge of sending to a far different neighborhood, reflecting bitterly on one sure reality: cemeteries are filled with curious people. But he was no less sure that after the incident with the Italian, and with the two masked men and Fray Emilio Bocanegra awaiting results, the possibility of the cemetery was not a "perhaps." So staying, leaving, or dancing a chaconne was all one and the same. Sticking his head in the sand, like that rare bird from Africa, would not solve any-thing, and furthermore, it was not Diego Alatriste's nature. He was aware that in blocking the Italian's sword he had taken a definitive step, and there was no turning back. Thus the only remedy was to play the hand with the cards dealt by that old joker Destiny, even though they were terrible.

He looked at the two young Englishmen. By this time, according to the agreement—the one he was carrying gold in his purse for executing—they should be cold cuts on a platter. He felt drops of sweat trickle down the back of his neck. What a whore luck was, he cursed silently. A fine moment he'd chosen to play at being a gentleman and suf-fer a crisis of conscience in some alleyway in Madrid—an old girl on her way down. And he with her.

The Englishman dressed in gray was on his feet and look-ing at the captain. Now it was his turn to be studied by Alatriste in the light of the lantern: blond, curling mus-tache, elegant air, circles of fatigue beneath his blue eyes. Barely thirty, and obviously well-bred. And like his friend, pale as wax. There had been no color in their faces since Alatriste and the Italian fell upon them.

"We are in your debt," said the man in gray, and after a brief pause he added, "In spite of everything."

His Spanish was riddled with imperfections, with the strong accent of "those up there," that is, the English. His tone seemed sincere. It was evident that he and his companion had seen death face to face, with no soft lights or heroic drumrolls, but in the dark, and nearly in the back, like rats in an alleyway and several leagues from anything remotely resembling glory. An encounter that few members of the upper classes had experienced, accustomed as they were to departing this mortal coil amid fifes and drums, serene as the elegant profile on a coin. The fact is that from time to time he blinked without taking his gaze from the captain's, as if surprised to find himself alive. And the truth was that now he was going to live, heretic or no.

"In spite of everything," the heretic repeated.

The captain did not know what to say. After all, despite the denouement of the ambush, he and his soldier-of-fortune companion had intended to murder the two Misters Smith, or whoever these bastards were. To fill the embarrassing pause, the captain glanced away, and the glint of the Englishman's sword caught his eye. He walked over, picked it up, and returned it to him. The so-called Thomas Smith, or Steenie—and what the devil kind of name was *that?*—weighed it pensively before putting it back in its scabbard. He kept looking at Alatriste with those frank blue eyes that made the captain feel so uneasy.

"At the beginning we thought . . ." the Englishman said, then waited as though expecting Alatriste to complete his sentence. The captain merely shrugged. At that moment the wounded youth made a move to get up, and "Steenie" turned to help. Both men's swords were now sheathed, and in what little light remained they observed the captain speculatively.

"You are not a common thief," said Steenie, who slowly was recovering his color.

Alatriste glanced toward the young man whom his companion had several times addressed as "Milord." Thin blond mustache, fine hands, aristocratic-looking despite the clothing stiff with the dust and filth of the road. If that individual was not from a good family, the captain would pledge himself to the faith of the Turks. By his life he would.

"Your name?" the man in gray asked.

It truly was amazing that these heretics were still alive, for they were innocent as lambs. Or perhaps that was the reason they were. All Alatriste could do was stay silent. He was not a man given to confidences, even less one to spill his feelings to two strangers he had been about to kill. So he could not, God knows, imagine what made this dandified young stranger think he was going to open his heart to him, just to be a good fellow. In any case, despite how much he wanted to find out what the fuck this was all about, the captain began to think that it might be better to put a little distance between himself and the two men. Getting into questions and answers was not something that suited him in the least. Besides, someone might appear at any moment: the watchman making his rounds or . . . Anything unexpected could complicate things. Indeed, given the worst possibility, it might occur to the Italian, whistling his *ti-ri-tu, ta-ta,* to return with reinforcements to get the job done. That thought made the captain take a worried look down the dark lane behind him. He had to get out of there, and quickly.

"Who sent you?" the Englishman insisted.

Without answering, Alatriste went to retrieve his cape. He threw it over one shoulder, leaving the hand that wielded his sword free, just in case. The horses were close by, dragging their reins on the ground.

"Get on your horses and go," he said.

The one called Steenie did not move, but turned to consult with his companion, who had not spoken a word in Spanish and seemed to have only a rudimentary comprehension of it. They exchanged a few phrases in their tongue, speaking very low, and the wounded youth nodded. At last the one in gray spoke to Alatriste.

"You were going to kill me, but you relented," he said. "You also saved my friend's life. Why?"

"Old age. I am turning soft."

The Englishman shook his head. "This was not a chance encounter." He looked toward his companion and then at the captain, with sharpened attention. "Someone hired you, is that not true?"

The captain was beginning to lose patience answering so many questions, and even more when he saw that his questioner's hand was moving toward the purse at his waist, suggesting that any helpful word would be generously remunerated. At that Alatriste frowned, twisted his mustache, and placed his hand on the pommel of his sword.

"Look at me carefully, Your Mercy," he said. "Do I look like someone who tells his life story to anyone who happens along?"

The Englishman stared at him, hard, and slowly removed his hand from his purse. "No," he conceded. In truth you do not."

Alatriste nodded approvingly. "I am very happy that you agree with me. Now fetch your horses and get out of here. My companion may return."

"And you, sir?"

"That is my affair."

Again the two young men exchanged words in English. The one in gray seemed to be considering something, elbow cupped in one hand, chin on fist. An unusual stance, notably affected, more suitable to the elegant palaces of

London than to a dark lane in Madrid. In him, however, it seemed natural, as if he were accustomed to striking a pose. So white and so blond, he had the air of a popinjay, or a courtier, but it was also true that he had fought with skill and courage, just as his companion had. Their patterns of behavior, the captain observed, were cut from the same cloth. A pair of well-bred youths, he concluded. In over their heads with women, religion, or politics. Or perhaps all three.

"No one must know about this," the Englishman said at last.

A quiet laugh escaped Diego Alatriste. "I am not the most eager among us to have it known."

The youth seemed surprised by the captain's laugh, or perhaps he did not fully understand what he said; but after a moment he, too, smiled. A faint, courteous smile. A bit superior.

"There is much at stake," he added.

The captain was in complete agreement. "My head," he murmured. "For example."

If the Englishman captured the irony, he paid scant attention. Again he struck his thoughtful pose.

"My friend needs to rest a little. And the man who wounded him could be waiting for us farther down the lane." Again he made a point of studying the man before him, attempting to measure from his attitude how sincere or how deceitful he was. In the end, he raised his eyebrows, suggesting that neither he nor his companion had many choices.

"Do you, sir, know our final destination?"

Alatriste met his gaze without blinking. "I may."

"Do you know the House of Seven Chimneys?"

"Perhaps."

"Will you take us there?"

"No."

"Would you take a message for us?"

"Not a chance."

This man must take me for an imbecile, he thought. That was exactly what he needed: Walk right into the wolf's mouth and alert the English ambassador and his servants. Curiosity killed the cat, he reminded himself as he glanced around uneasily. Now was the moment to be thinking of saving his skin, which more than one person was eager to perforate. Yes, it was time to look after himself, time to put an end to the conversation. But the Englishman stopped him.

"Do you know of any place nearby where we might find help? Or rest awhile?"

Alatriste was going to say no for the last time, before fading into the shadows, when an idea flooded his mind like sunlight bursting from the clouds. He himself had nowhere to hide, for the Italian and others sent by the masked men and Padre Bocanegra would come to look for him at his lodgings on Calle del Arcabuz, where at that hour I was sleeping like a dormouse. But no one would harm me; *his* gullet, on the other hand, would be slit before he had time to pick up his sword. This might be an opportunity to secure protection for the night and help for what lay ahead. At the same time he would be aiding the Englishmen, finding out more about them and about the men who were so eager to see them leave this earth.

The card up his sleeve, one Diego Alatriste tried not to play too often, was named Álvaro de la Marca, Conde de Guadalmedina. And his palatial home was only a hundred steps away.

"This is a fine fix you have got yourself into."

Álvaro Luis Gonzaga de la Marca y Álvarez de Sidonia, Conde de Guadalmedina, was handsome, elegant, and so rich that he could lose ten thousand ducats at cards in one night, or squander it on one of his lady friends, without lifting an eyebrow. At the time of the adventure of the two Englishmen, he must have been about thirty-three or thirty-four, in the prime of his life. Son of the now deceased Conde de Guadalmedina—don Fernando Gonzaga de la Marca, hero of the Flemish campaigns in the time of the great Philip the Second and his heir Philip the Third—

Álvaro de la Marca had inherited from his progenitor the title of grandee of Spain, along with the right to wear his hat in the presence of the young monarch, the fourth Philip, whose friendship he enjoyed, and whom, it was said, he accompanied on nocturnal amorous escapades with the actresses and beauties of low estate favored by both king and count.

Bachelor, womanizer, courtier, sophisticate, a bit of a poet, a gallant, and a seducer, Guadalmedina had bought from the king the sinecure of Master of the Post upon the recent and scandalous death of the previous beneficiary, the Conde de Villamediana (a point of caution here: he himself murdered over a matter of skirts, or jealousy). In that corrupt Spain in which everything could be bought, from ecclesiastical dignity to the most lucrative state positions, the title and the income of Master of the Post swelled Guadalmedina's fortune and influence at court. In addition, as a youth he had gained prestige in his brief but brilliant military career, when at twenty-some years of age he had served on the staff of the Duque de Osuna, fighting against the Venetians and the Turks on Spanish galleys that sailed out of Naples. It was precisely from those days that his acquaintance with Diego Alatriste dated.

"A devilishly fine fix," Guadalmedina repeated.

The captain had no response. He was hatless and without his cape, standing in a small salon decorated with

Flemish tapestries, and beside him, on a table covered with green velvet, was a glass of liquor he had not tasted. Guadalmedina, dressed in an exquisite jacket and satin slippers, was frowning and pacing back and forth before the fire, thinking about what Alatriste had just told him. It was the true story of what had happened, step by step—with only one or two omissions—from the episode with the masked men to the denouement of the ambush in the alley. The count was one of the few men the captain trusted blindly, though, as he had decided when he led the two Englishmen to the count's dwelling, that was an honor for which there was not much competition.

"Do you know these men you intended to kill?"

"No. No, I do not." Alatriste chose his words with supreme care. "In principle, one Thomas Smith and his companion. At least that is what they tell me. Or told me."

"*Who* told you?"

"That is what I would like to know."

Álvaro de la Marca had stopped before him and was looking at him with a mixture of admiration and reproach. The captain merely nodded slightly, and he heard the aristocrat murmur, "All the saints above," before he again paced the length of the room.

At that moment, the count's servants, who had been quickly mobilized, were attending the Englishmen in the best room of the house. While Alatriste was waiting, he had

heard the sounds of scurrying footsteps, opening and closing doors, servants at the gate, and neighing in the stables,
where, through the mansion's leaded windows, he could see
the glow of torches. The house seemed to be preparing for
war. The count had written urgent messages in his office
before joining Alatriste. Despite his host's sangfroid and his
habitual good humor, the captain had seldom seen him
so agitated.

"So . . . Thomas Smith," the count said quietly.

"That is what they said."

"Thomas Smith. Just that, nothing more."

"Correct."

Guadalmedina faced him again.

"Thomas Smith, my left pinky," he spit out impatiently.
"The one in the gray suit is named George Villiers. You
have heard the name?" Brusquely he swept up the glass
Alatriste had not touched, and downed it in one gulp.
"Better known throughout Europe by his English title: the
Marquis of Buckingham."

A man with a less even keel than Diego Alatriste y
Tenorio, former soldier in the regiments that fought in
Flanders, would have looked desperately for a chair to sit
down in. Or to be more exact, to drop into. But the captain
stood square, meeting Guadalmedina's eyes as if this had
nothing to do with him. Much later, however, over a jar of
wine and with only me as witness, the captain would ac-

knowledge that he had had to anchor his thumbs in his waistband to keep his hands from shaking, and that his head had begun to spin like a whirligig at a fair. The Marquis of Buckingham; everyone in Spain knew who that was. The youthful favorite of King James the First of England, the cream of English nobility, famous gentleman and elegant courtier, adored by the ladies and destined for a leading role in His Britannic Majesty's affairs of state. Only a few weeks later, during his stay in Madrid, he would be made a duke.

"To sum up," Guadalmedina concluded acidly. "You were on the verge of murdering the favorite of the King of England. As for the other one . . ."

"John Smith?"

This time there was a note of resigned humor in Diego Alatriste's voice. Guadalmedina had clapped his hands to his head, and the captain observed that the mere mention of Mister John Smith, whoever the man was, had made the aristocrat turn pale. A moment or two later, Álvaro de la Marca ran his thumbnail through his goatee and looked the captain up and down once more, this time with admiration.

"You are incredible, Alatriste." He took two steps, stopped again, and looked at the captain with the same expression. "*In*credible."

To use the word "friendship" would be an exaggeration in defining the relationship between Guadalmedina and the former soldier, but we could speak of mutual appreciation—within the limits of both men. Álvaro de la Marca felt sincere esteem for the captain. That tale had begun when in his youth Diego Alatriste served with distinction in Flanders, fighting under the flags of the old Conde de Guadalmedina, who had more than one opportunity to demonstrate his fondness and appreciation. Later, the fortunes of war had brought the two together, in Naples, and though Alatriste was a simple soldier, he had rendered the son of his former general some services during the disastrous day of the Kerkennah Islands. Álvaro de la Marca had not forgotten, and when, after inheriting fortune and titles he had exchanged his weapons for life at court, he did not turn away from the captain. From time to time he hired his services as a swordsman: to collect debts, to escort him on romantic and dangerous adventures, or to settle accounts with cuckolded husbands, rivals in love, and annoying creditors. That, incidentally, had been the case with the young Marqués de Soto at the Acero fountain, to whom, we remember, following Guadalmedina's prescription, Alatriste had administered a lethal dose of steel.

But far from taking advantage of that information, with which a good number of the arrogant sycophants who hung around at court seeking a benefice or doubloons would have made hay, Diego Alatriste kept his distance, never coming to the count except on occasions of absolute and desperate need, such as this. Something which, in addition, he would never have done had he not been sure of the nobility of the men he had attacked. And the gravity of what was about to befall him.

"Are you sure that you did not recognize either of the two masked men who charged you with this commission?"

"I have told Your Mercy. They seemed respectable men, but I was not able to identify either."

Guadalmedina again stroked his goatee. "There were only two of them that night?"

"Two that I recall."

"And one said to let them live, and the other said to kill them."

"More or less."

The count was staring hard at Alatriste. "By my oath! You are hiding something, sir!"

The captain shrugged, holding his protector's gaze. "Perhaps," he replied calmly.

Álvaro de la Marca smiled sarcastically, his scrutiny of Alatriste never lessening. They both knew that Alatriste was not going to say a word more than he already had, even if the count threatened to wash his hands of the matter and put him out on the street.

"Very well," he concluded. "After all, it is your neck."

The captain nodded fatalistically. One of the few omissions in the tale told to the count was the role of Fray Emilio Bocanegra. Not because Alatriste had any wish to protect the Inquisitor—who was more to be feared than to be protected—but because, in spite of Alatriste's boundless faith in Guadalmedina, he was not an informer. It was one thing to tell about the masked men, but something else again to denounce the persons who had given him employ, no matter that one of them was the Dominican priest, and that the whole story, and its outcome, might cause Alatriste himself to end up in the less than friendly care of the executioner. The captain was repaying the aristocrat's kindness to him by placing the fate of those Englishmen in his hands—and his along with theirs. But although he was an old soldier and a hired sword, he too had his twisted codes. He was not prepared to break them, even if it cost him his life, and Guadalmedina knew that very well. There had been times when Álvaro de la Marca's name was the one to be given up, but with equal poise the captain had refused to reveal it to questioners. In the limited portion of the world that the two men shared despite their very different lives, those were the rules. And Guadalmedina was not prepared to infringe on them, not even with the Marquis of Buckingham and his companion sitting in his home. It was evident from his expression that Álvaro de la Marca was calculating as quickly as possible the best use he could make of the state secret that chance and Diego Alatriste had placed in his hands.

A servant was standing respectfully at the door. The count went to him, and Diego Alatriste heard them exchange a few words in low voices. When the domestic retired, Guadalmedina returned to the captain, looking thoughtful.

"I had advised the English ambassador, but those gentlemen say that it is not desirable for the meeting to take place in my home. So since they have rested, I will have several men I can trust, and me along with them, escort our two guests to the House of Seven Chimneys, to spare them further unpleasant encounters."

"May I do anything to help Your Mercy?"

The count looked at him with ironic irritation. "I fear that you have already done enough for today. The most helpful thing you can do is to stay out of it."

Alatriste nodded, and with a private sigh, resigned, slowly started to leave. Clearly, he could not return home, or take refuge with any close friend, and if Guadalmedina did not offer him lodging, he would be forced to roam the streets at the mercy of his enemies or the constables of Martín Saldaña, who might already have been alerted. The count knew all that. He knew also that Diego Alatriste would never ask directly for help; he was too proud. If Guadalmedina did not acknowledge the tacit message, the captain had no choice but to face his fate in the street, with no resources but his sword. But the count was smiling, drawn from his thoughts.

"You may stay here this night," he said. "And tomorrow we shall see what life has in store. I have ordered that a room be prepared for you."

Imperceptibly, Alatriste relaxed. Through the half-open door he saw the aristocrat's servants laying out clothing. He watched as two of them brought an old buffcoat and several loaded pistols. Álvaro de la Marca did not seem inclined to expose his unexpected guests to further risk.

"Within a few hours the news of these gentlemen's arrival will have spread, and all Madrid will be abuzz." The count sighed. "They ask me as a gentleman to keep secret the news of the ambush that you and your companion prepared for them, and also ask that no one know that you helped them find refuge here. All this is very delicate, Alatriste. And more than your neck is involved. Officially, their trip ended without incident at the home of the English ambassador. And that is where we are going to attempt to go right now."

The count was moving toward the room where his clothing awaited, when suddenly he appeared to remember something.

"Oh," he added, pausing, "they wish to see you before they go. I do not know how in the devil you came to a peaceful resolution, but after I told them who you are, and how the thing came about, they did not seem to hold too much rancor. Those English and their damned British phlegm! I swear by God and all that is holy that if you had given me the fright you gave them, I would be yelling for your head. I would not have lost a minute in having you murdered."

The interview was brief, and took place in the enormous vestibule beneath a canvas by Titian that showed Danaë on the verge of being impregnated by Zeus in the form of a shower of gold. Álvaro de la Marca, now dressed and equipped as if he planned to assault a Turkish galley, with several pistol grips showing above his waist sash, along with his sword and dagger, led the captain to the place where the Englishmen were waiting to leave, wrapped in their capes and surrounded by the count's servants, they, too, armed to the teeth. Only the drums were lacking to complete their resemblance to a night patrol of soldiers on the eve of a skirmish.

"Here you have your man," said Guadalmedina sarcastically, indicating the captain.

The Englishmen had cleaned up and rested from their journey. Their clothing had been brushed and was reasonably presentable, and the younger man was wearing a folded cloth around his neck, supporting the arm on the side of his injury. The other Englishman, the one in gray, whom Álvaro de la Marca had identified as Buckingham, had recovered an arrogance that Alatriste did not recall having seen during the fracas in the lane.

George Villiers, Marquis of Buckingham, was already the Lord High Admiral of the English fleet and enjoyed considerable influence in the circle around King James the First. He was ambitious, intelligent, romantic, and adventurous, and it would be only a brief time before he received the ducal title by which history and legend would know him. Now, still young, and quickly ascending toward the highest levels in the Court of Saint James's, he showed obvious annoyance as he stared at his attacker, but Alatriste bore his inspection without wincing. Marquis, archbishop, or villain, this fine-looking fellow brought neither heat nor chill to the captain, be he favorite of King James or first cousin to the pope. It was Fray Emilio Bocanegra and the two masked men who would keep Alatriste from sleeping that night and, he feared, for many more.

"You came close to killing us tonight in the lane," the Englishman said very serenely in his heavily accented Spanish, addressing himself more to Guadalmedina than to Alatriste.

"I regret what happened," the captain replied evenly, with a nod. "But we are not all privileged to do as we will with our swords."

The Englishman stared at him a few instants longer. Scorn was apparent in his blue eyes; all the surprise and spontaneity of the first moments after the struggle in the lane had vanished. He had had time to think things over, and the recollection of having found himself at the mercy of an unknown swordsman wounded his self-esteem. Thence the newly emerged arrogance, which Alatriste had not so much as glimpsed when they crossed blades earlier in the lantern light.

"I believe we are even," Buckingham said after a moment. And turning abruptly, he began to put on his gloves.

Beside him, the younger Englishman, the purported John Smith, his brow clear, white, and noble, his features finely chiseled, stood in silence. Despite the traveling clothes, the delicate hands and elegant stance betrayed from afar that he was a young man of distinguished family. Beneath his smooth mustache the captain glimpsed the suggestion of a smile. Alatriste nodded again and was about to leave, when the still-unidentified man spoke a few words in his language that made his companion turn toward him. Out of the corner of his eye, Alatriste saw Guadalmedina smile: in addition to French and Latin, he spoke the heretics' tongue.

"My friend says that he owes you his life." George Villiers appeared uncomfortable. As far as he was concerned, the conversation was clearly closed, but grudgingly he translated the younger man's words. "He says that the last thrust from the man in black would have been lethal."

"Possibly." Alatriste, too, allowed himself a slight smile. "We all were blessed tonight, I believe."

The Englishman finished fitting on his gloves as he listened carefully to what his companion told him.

"My friend would like to know what it was that made you reconsider and change sides."

"I have not changed sides," said Alatriste. "I am always on my own. I hunt alone."

As his friend translated, the younger man studied the captain thoughtfully. Suddenly, he seemed more mature and more authoritative than his companion. The captain had observed that even Guadalmedina deferred to him more than he did to Buckingham. Then the younger man spoke again, and his companion protested in their language, as if he did not agree that he should translate those last words. But his friend insisted, with a tone of authority that Alatriste had not heard from him before.

"The gentleman says," Buckingham translated, unwillingly, in his broken Spanish, "that it does not matter who you are or what your office may be, only that you acted nobly when you saved him from being killed like a common dog, a victim of treachery. He says that despite everything, he considers himself in your debt and wants you to know . . . He says . . ." The translator hesitated a moment and exchanged a worried glance with Guadalmedina before he continued. "He says that tomorrow all Europe will know that the son and heir of King James of England is in Madrid with the sole escort and company of his friend the Marquis of Buckingham. . . . And he says that though for reasons of state it is impossible to publish what happened tonight, he, Charles, Prince of Wales, future King of England, Scotland, and Ireland, will never forget that a man named Diego Alatriste could have killed him, but chose not to."

VI. THE ART OF MAKING ENEMIES

The next morning Madrid awakened to the incredible news. Charles Stuart, cub of the English lion, impatient with the pace of matrimonial negotiations with the Infanta doña María, sister of our King Philip the Fourth, had with his friend Buckingham conceived this extraordinary and preposterous project of traveling to Madrid, incognito, to meet his future bride. In so doing, he hoped to transform the cold diplomatic exchanges that had been languishing for months in the chancelleries into a novel of chivalric love.

The marriage between the Anglican prince and the Catholic princess had at this point become a complicated imbroglio in which ambassadors, diplomats, ministers, foreign governments, and even His Holiness the Roman Pope were caught up. The pope would have to authorize the union and was, of course, angling for the largest slice of this tasty pie. So, impatient that no one was flushing his partridge—or whatever those accursed English hunt—the Prince of Wales, seconded by Buckingham, had with his boyish imagination devised a plan to hasten negotiations. Between them they had plotted, confident that traveling to Spain without notice or protocol would immediately conquer the Infanta, and they would carry her off to England before the astonished gaze of all of Europe, and with the applause and approval of the Spanish and English peoples.

That, more or less, was the heart of the matter. Once King James's initial resistance had been overcome, he gave both youths his benediction and authorized them to set out. Though the risk of his son's undertaking was great—an accident, failure, or a Spanish rebuff would put England's honor on the line—the advantages of achieving a happy ending balanced the risk. First of all, to have the monarch of the nation that was still the most powerful in the world as brother-in-law to his heir was not a small thing. In addition, the marriage, desired by the English court but received more coolly by the Conde de Olivares and the ultra-Catholic counselors of the King of Spain, would put an end to the old enmity between the two nations. Consider, Your Mercies, that barely thirty years had gone by since the defeat of the Invincible Armada; and you know how that went, with cannon shot here and the briny deep there. Yes, the Devil takes all, in that fatal arm-wrestling contest between our good King don Philip the Second and that redheaded harpy named Elizabeth of England, harborer of Protestants, bastards, and pirates, and better known as the Virgin Queen, though be damned if it is possible to imagine her Virgin anything.

The fact is that a wedding between the young heretic and our infanta—who was no Venus but was not all that bad, if you go by how Diego Velázquez painted her a little later, young and blonde, a lady . . . with that very Hapsburg lip, of course—would peacefully open the ports of commerce in the West Indies to England, resolving the burning problem of the Palatinate in favor of the British. That is a story I do not choose to go into here, because that is what history tomes are for.

So that is how the cards had been dealt the night that I was sleeping like a dormouse on my pallet in Calle del Arcabuz, unaware of what was brewing, while Captain Alatriste, with one hand on the grip of his pistol, and his sword within reach of the other, spent sleepless hours in a servant's room in the Conde de Guadalmedina's mansion. As for Charles Stuart and Buckingham, they lodged in considerably greater comfort, and with every honor, in the home of the English ambassador. The following morning, when the news had spread and while the counselors of our lord and king, with the Conde de Olivares at their head, attempted to seek a way out of the diplomatic crisis, the people of Madrid gathered en masse before the House of Seven Chimneys to cheer the daring traveler.

Charles Stuart was young, ardent, and optimistic. He had recently turned twenty-two, and, with that aplomb the young have in copious supply, he was as sure of the seductiveness of his gesture as he was of the love of an infanta whom he had never met. He was similarly sure, counting on our reputation for being gentlemanly and hospitable, that the Spanish, along with his lady, would be conquered by such a gallant gesture. And in that he was correct.

Yes, if the nearly half-century reign of our good and ineffective monarch don Philip the Fourth, mistakenly called the Great—all chivalry and hospitality, mass on holidays, parading around with splendor and sword and empty belly—had filled Spain's coffers and put pikemen in Flanders, it is also true that I, my captain Alatriste, the Spanish in general, and poor Spain in all its kingdoms had danced to a different tune. And that infamous period was called the Siglo de Oro? *What* Golden Age, eh? The truth is that those of us who lived and suffered through it saw little gold and barely enough silver. Sterile sacrifice, glorious defeats, corruption, rogues, misery, and shame, *that* we had up to the eyebrows. But then when one goes and looks at a painting by Diego Velázquez, listens to verses by Lope or Calderón, reads a sonnet by Francisco de Quevedo, one says to oneself that perhaps it was all worthwhile.

But back to my tale. I was telling you that the news of the adventure raced around the city like a trail of gunpowder, and won the heart of all Madrid, though for our lord and king and the Conde de Olivares, as we later learned, the uninvited arrival of the heir to the English crown had hit them like lead shot between the eyes. Protocol was maintained, of course, and everything was all consideration and compliments. And of the skirmish in the lane, not so much as a whisper.

Diego Alatriste learned the particulars when the Conde de Guadalmedina returned home early in the morning, happy over the success he had just scored by escorting the two young men and being the recipient of their gratitude and that of the English ambassador. After the obligatory courtesies in the House of Seven Chimneys, Guadalmedina had been urgently summoned to the Royal Palace, where he brought the king and first minister up-to-date on the happenings. Bound by his word, the count could not reveal the details of the ambush. But without incurring the displeasure of the king, on the one hand, or betraying his word as a gentleman, on the other, Álvaro de la Marca knew how to communicate enough details through gestures, hints, and silences, that the monarch and his prime minister comprehended, to their horror, how close the two imprudent travelers had come to being filleted in a dark lane in Madrid.

The full story, or at least some of the key points that were enough to give Diego Alatriste an idea of who his shadowy employers were, came from Guadalmedina's mouth. After spending half the morning traveling back and forth between the House of Seven Chimneys and the palace, he brought fresh, though not especially calming, news for the captain.

"In truth, it is very simple," the count summarized. "For some time, England has been pressing for this marriage, but Olivares and the Council, which is still under his influence, are in no hurry. That an infanta of Castile should marry an Anglican prince brought the smell of sulfur to their nostrils. The king is young, and in this, as in everything else, he lets himself be guided by Olivares. Those within the close personal circle of the king believe that the prime minister has no intention of giving his stamp of approval to the wedding—unless the Prince of Wales should convert to Catholicism. That is why Olivares has been dragging his feet, and that is also why the young Charles decided to take the bull by the horns and present us with a fait accompli."

. . .

Álvaro de la Marca was sitting at the green-velvet-covered table, wolfing down a small snack. It was mid-morning, and they were in the same room in which he had received Diego Alatriste the night before. The aristocrat was giving his devoted attention to a chicken *empanada*, meat pies being one of his favorite dishes, and drinking wine from a small silver jug; his diplomatic and social success the night before had clearly whetted his appetite. He had invited Alatriste to join him at table, but the captain rejected the invitation. He remained standing, leaning against the wall, watching his protector eat. Alatriste was dressed to go out; his cape, sword, and hat were on a nearby chair, and his unshaven face showed traces of his sleepless night.

"Your Mercy, who do you think is most disturbed by the idea of this marriage?"

Between bites, Guadalmedina looked up. "Oof. Many people." He set the *empanada* on the plate and began to count on fingers shiny with grease.

"In Spain, the Church and the Inquisition are soundly against it. To them you would have to add that the pope, France, Savoy, and Venice are still open to anything that would impede an alliance between England and Spain. Can you imagine what would have happened if you had succeeded in killing the prince and Buckingham?"

"War with England, I suppose."

Again the count attacked his food. "You suppose correctly." He nodded somberly. "At the moment there is general agreement that the incident should be kept quiet. The prince and Buckingham maintain that they were the object of an attack by common footpads, and the king and Olivares are acting as if they believe them. Afterward, when they were alone, the king asked the prime minister to conduct an investigation, and he promised to see to it immediately." Guadalmedina paused to take a long swallow of wine, then dried his mustache and goatee with an enormous napkin rustling with starch. "Knowing Olivares, I am sure that he himself was *capable* of setting up an ambush, although I do not think he would go that far. The truce with Holland is falling through, and it would be absurd to distract from the war effort by taking on an unnecessary conflict with England."

The count finished off the *empanada*, staring distractedly at the Flemish tapestry on the wall behind the captain: horsemen attacking a castle, and hostile individuals in turbans aiming arrows and stones at them from the merlons. The tapestry had been hanging there for more than thirty years, ever since the old general, don Fernando de la Marca, took it as booty during the last sacking of Antwerp, in the glorious days of the great King Philip. Now don Fernando's son was slowly chewing and staring at it reflectively. He turned to look at Alatriste.

"Those masked men who hired your services could be paid agents for Venice, Savoy, France, or who knows where. . . . Are you sure they were Spanish?"

"As Spanish as you or I. And men of breeding."

"Do not put your faith in breeding. Here everyone claims to be from an old Christian family, a gentleman, someone of stature. Yesterday I had to dismiss my barber, who had the brass to try to shave me while his sword hung at his waist. Even servants carry them. And as work degrades honor, not even Christ lifts a hand."

"But these I speak of were gentlemen. And Spanish."

"Very well. Spanish or not, it is all the same. As if a foreigner could not pay someone to carry out his underhanded schemes." The aristocrat laughed a bitter little laugh. "In this Hapsburg Spain, my dear fellow, the gold of nobleman and villain alike is equally welcome. Everything is for sale, except the nation's honor; and even that we secretly barter at the first opportunity. As for the rest, what can I tell you? Our conscience . . ." He looked at the captain over the silver jug. "Our swords . . ."

"And our souls," Alatriste finished with a flourish.

Guadalmedina took another sip, never removing his eyes from the captain.

"Yes," he said. "Your masked men could even be in the pay of our good pontiff, Gregory. Our Holy Father cannot abide the sight of a Spaniard."

The fire in the great stone-and-marble hearth had burned down, and the sun shining through the windows was barely warm, but that mention of the Church was enough to make Diego Alatriste feel uncomfortably flushed. The sinister image of Fray Emilio Bocanegra floated through his mind like a specter. He had spent the night seeing him materialize on the dark ceiling of the room, in the shadows of the trees outside the window, in the dark corridor, and the light of day was not bright enough to make him fade completely. Guadalmedina's words brought him back again, like a bad omen.

"Whoever they may be," the count continued, "their objective is clear: to avert the marriage, to teach a terrible lesson to England, and to see war explode between the two nations. And you, by changing your mind, poleaxed everything. You earned your degree in the art of making enemies, so, were I you, I would take good care to guard my back. The problem is that I cannot protect you any longer. With you here, I myself could become implicated. Again, if I were in your shoes, I would take a long journey . . . a very long journey. . . . And whatever it is you know, do not tell anyone, even in confession. If a priest learned anything of this, he would hang up his habit, sell the secret, and live life as a wealthy man."

"And what about the Englishman? Is he safe now?"

Guadalmedina assured Alatriste that he was. With all Europe knowing where he was, the Englishman could consider himself as safe as if he were in his foul Tower of London. It was one thing for Olivares and the king to keep dragging their feet, to lionize the prince and make promise after promise, until he got bored and followed a fair wind home. It was altogether different to claim that they could not guarantee his safety.

"Besides," the count went on, "Olivares is wily, and he knows how to improvise. He can easily change his plan, and the king with him. Do you know what he told the prince this morning in my presence? That if they did not obtain dispensation from Rome and could not give him the infanta as a wife, they would give her to him as a lover. A fine one, that Olivares! A whoreson to end all whoresons—clever and dangerous, and sharper than the pangs of hunger. And Charles, completely content now, is sure that he will hold doña María in his arms."

"Does anyone know how she feels about the matter?"

"She is young, so use your imagination. She is not averse to love. That a young, handsome heretic of royal blood would do what he did for her both repels and fascinates her. But she is an infanta of Castile, so protocol is to be observed. I doubt that they will let them anywhere near each other, even to pray an Ave Maria. And by the way, just as I was coming home, I composed the first lines of a little sonnet.

"Wales came to seek his infanta fair
And a bridal bed, but if truth be told,
The coveted prize, the Lion learned,
Goes to the patient, not the bold."

"What do you think?" Álvaro de la Marca looked at Alatriste, who was smiling lightly, amused but prudently abstaining from comment.

"I am not Lope, forsooth! And I imagine that your friend Quevedo would make some serious objections, but for something of mine, it is not at all bad. If you come across it on one of those anonymous broadsheets, you will know whose it is. . . . Well, then."

The count downed the rest of his wine and stood, tossing his napkin on the table. "Getting back to serious questions, one thing is true: An alliance with England would put us in a better position regarding France. After the Protestants—I would say even more than those dissenters—that is our principal threat in Europe. We must hope that over time Olivares and the king will change their minds and the wedding will take place, although from the comments I heard from them in private, that would surprise me greatly."

The count walked aimlessly around the room, again examined the tapestry his father had stolen in Antwerp, and stopped, thoughtful, at the window.

"It might somehow have been understandable," he went on, "if an anonymous traveler, one who officially was not even here, had been the victim of an unknown swordsman last night. But now . . . If an attempt were made now on the life of the grandson of Mary Stuart, a guest of the King of Spain, and the future monarch of England . . . 'Sblood! That could not be as easily explained. The moment has passed. And for that reason I imagine that your masked men must be enraged, clamoring for vengeance. Furthermore, it is not in their best interest that there be witnesses who might speak out, and the best way to silence a witness is to fit him for a coffin."

Again his eyes bored into Alatriste's. "Do you understand your situation? Yes? I am happy to hear that. And now, Captain Alatriste, I have devoted too much time to you. I have things to do, among them completing my sonnet. You must look to your safety, and may God help you."

. . .

All Madrid was one great fiesta. The people's curiosity had converted the House of Seven Chimneys into a colorful place of pilgrimage. Large numbers of curious Madrileños followed Calle de Alcalá to the church of the Discalced Carmelites, passed it, and congregated before the residence of the English ambassador, where mild-mannered constables kept pushing back the spectators, who cheered every time one of the carriages going to or coming from the house passed. There were constant calls for the Prince of Wales to come out to greet them, and when at mid-morning a young blond appeared for a moment at one of the windows, he received a thunderous ovation, to which he replied with a wave of the hand so genteel that he immediately won the approval of the crowd gathered in the street.

Generous, sympathetic, welcoming to anyone who knew how to reach their hearts, the people of Madrid would show to the heir of the English throne the same evidence of their appreciation and goodwill during all the months he was to spend at court. The history of our benighted Spain would have been very different had the generous impulses of the people won out more frequently over the arid doctrine of the state and the self-interest, venality, and ineptitude of our politicians, nobles, and monarchs. The anonymous chronicler who composed the ballad of *El*

Cid says the same of the ordinary people of that day. His words come to mind when one considers the sad history of our people, who always have given the best of themselves—their innocence, their money, their labors, and their blood—only to find themselves ill repaid in return: *"What a fine vassal would he have made, had he but served a good lord."*

The case is that the Madrileños came that morning to celebrate the Prince of Wales, and I myself was there accompanying Caridad la Lebrijana, who did not want to miss the spectacle. I do not know whether I have told you, but at that time La Lebrijana was about thirty or thirty-five years old, a common but beautiful Andalusian, still spirited and well formed; she had olive skin, large black shining eyes, and a generous bosom. For five or six years she had been an actress, and about that many more a whore in a house on Calle de las Huertas. Weary of that life, at the first sign of crow's-feet she had used her savings to buy the Tavern of the Turk, and with that asset she was now living in relative decency and comfort. I will add, and this is no secret, that La Lebrijana was painfully in love with my master Alatriste. Under that binding indenture she guaranteed him bread and drink, and also—because of the situation of the captain's lodgings, which communicated via the same courtyard with the back door of the tavern and the dwelling of La Lebrijana—a certain frequency in sharing of beds. I must make it clear that the captain was always very discreet in my presence, but when you live with another person, some things cannot be hidden. And though I may still have been a little wet behind the ears, I was not a ninny.

That day, as I was telling Your Mercies, I accompanied Caridad la Lebrijana up Mayor, Montera, and Alcalá to the residence of the English ambassador, where we joined the throng cheering the prince, along with all the other idlers and assorted humanity drawn there by curiosity. The street was buzzing louder than the steps of San Felipe, and vendors were offering water and mead, meat pies and conserves. Street stalls had been hastily set up where a morning's hunger could be satisfied for a few coins; beggars were busy, servants, pages, and squires were scurrying about, creating an uproar, and tit and tittle and fabulous invention swirled through the crowd like the wind. Events and rumors from the palace were parroted in group after group, and the aplomb and chivalric daring of the young prince were praised to the heavens. Tongues—especially those of the women—were wagging over his elegance and bearing, as well as other virtues of the prince and his friend Buckingham. And so the morning raced by in a very lively, very Spanish manner.

"How well he carries himself!" said La Lebrijana, after someone presumed to be the prince was seen at a window.

"A fine figure of a man, and such grace. He would make a great match for our infanta!"

She dried her tears with the tail of her shawl. Like most of the female spectators, she was on the side of the suitor. The audacity of his gesture had won hearts, and everyone considered the matter signed and sealed.

"What a shame that such a handsome fellow is a heretic. But a good confessor will remedy that, and in time, a baptism." In her ignorance, the woman believed that Anglicans were like the Turks, and were never baptized. "A bosom like a pouter pigeon will win out over any religion."

And she laughed, and the opulent bosom that so enthralled *me* quivered delectably, and in a certain way that I have great difficulty explaining, reminded me of my mother's. I can recall in every detail the sensation I felt every time Caridad la Lebrijana bent down to serve at table, and her blouse hinted of those great, mysterious, olive-skinned orbs, modeled by their own weight. Often I wondered what the captain might be doing with them those times that he sent me out to make a purchase, or to find something to do outside, leaving La Lebrijana and him alone in the house. As I ran down the steps two at a time, I would hear her laughing upstairs, very loud and very happy.

So there we were, enthusiastically cheering any figure

that appeared at a window, when Captain Alatriste came along. It was not the first night he had not come home, not by any stretch of the imagination, and I had slept the sleep of the dead, without a worry. But the minute I saw him at the House of Seven Chimneys, I sensed that something was wrong. His hat was pulled low over his face, his cape wrapped high around his neck, and his cheeks were not shaved despite the lateness of the hour, even though with his discipline as an old soldier he was always particular about how he looked. His gray-green eyes seemed tired and suspicious at the same time, and I watched him thread his way through the crowd with the wary attitude of someone who is expecting something bad to befall him at any moment.

Once I had assured him that no one had asked for him, neither during the night nor this morning, he seemed a bit more at ease. La Lebrijana said the same in regard to the tavern: no strangers, no inquiries. Later, when I moved a little apart, I heard her ask in a low voice what trouble he had gotten himself into this time. I took care to watch them, without appearing to, and kept my ears cocked, but Diego Alatriste said nothing more, only stared at the windows of the English ambassador's mansion, his expression unreadable.

Mixed in among the curious were people of quality: sedan chairs and coaches, including two or three carriages with ladies and their duennas peering between the curtains. I glanced at them through the itinerant vendors hurrying to offer them their wares, and thought I recognized one of the carriages. It was dark, with no coat of arms on the door, and had two good mules in the harness. The coachman was chatting with a group of bystanders, so I was able to approach the carriage without being run off. And there, at the little window, I needed only to see blue eyes and blond curls to confirm that my heart, which was pounding so madly I thought it might leap from my chest, had not erred.

"At your service," I said, controlling my voice with great effort.

I vow I do not know how, as young as Angélica de Alquézar was at the time, she—or anyone else—could learn to smile the way she smiled that morning in front of the House of Seven Chimneys. All I know is that she did. A slow smile, very slow, conveying both disdain and infinite wisdom. One of those smiles that no young girl has had time to learn in her brief life but that is born of the lucidity and penetrating gaze that is a female's exclusive territory, the fruit of centuries and centuries of silently observing men commit every manner of stupidity. I was too young to have learned how foolish we males can be, or how much can be learned from a woman's eyes and smile. No few misadventures in my adult life would have had a happier outcome had I devoted more time to that lesson. But no one is born wise, and often, just when a man is beginning to profit from such teachings, it is too late to benefit either health or fortunes.

The fact is that the girl with the blond curls and eyes like the cold, clear skies of a Madrid winter smiled when she recognized me; she even leaned slightly toward me, accompanied by the sound of rustling silk, and placed a small, delicate white hand on the window frame. I was right by the footboard of my lady's coach, and the euphoria of the morning and the atmosphere of chivalry surrounding us spurred my audacity. My self-confidence was reinforced by the fact that I had dressed that day with a certain decorum, thanks to a dark brown doublet and a pair of old hose that had belonged to Captain Alatriste but looked like new after I had fitted them to my size with Caridad la Lebrijana's needle and thread.

"Today there is no mud in the street," she said, and her voice shook me from my toes to the tip of my noggin. She spoke in a quiet, seductive tone; there was nothing childlike about it. Almost too serious for her age. Some ladies used that tone when addressing their gallants in the shows that strolling players presented in the plazas, and in the comedies in the theaters. But Angélica de Alquézar—whose name I did not yet know—was a young girl, not an actress. No one had taught her to feign that low throb in her voice, to enunciate her words in a way that made me feel like a grown man, and more . . . the only man for a thousand leagues around.

"No, there is no mud," I repeated, unaware of what I was saying. "And I regret that, for it prevents me from being of service again."

With those last words I placed my hand over my heart. You may conclude that I behaved rather well, and that the gallant reply and gesture were worthy of the lady and the circumstances. And it must have been so, because instead of turning away, she smiled again. And I was the happiest, the most gallant, the most hidalgo lad in the world.

"This is the page I spoke of," she said then, turning to someone beside her in the coach, whom I could not see. "His name is Íñigo, and he lives on Calle Arcabuz." Once more she turned toward me. I was staring at her open-mouthed, stunned that she had remembered my name. "With some captain, is that not true? A Captain Batiste, was it? Or Eltriste?"

There was a movement inside the coach, and first a hand with dirty fingernails, then a black-clad arm emerged from the dark carriage to rest on the window frame. They were followed by a cloak—that, too, black—and a doublet bearing the red insignia of the Order of Calatrava. And finally, above a narrow, badly starched ruff, appeared the face of a man in his late forties or early fifties. His head was round, the sparse hair coarse, the mustache and goatee dull and gray. Everything about him, despite his solemn garb, seemed somehow vulgar: common, unpleasant features, thick neck, ruddy nose, filthy hands, the way he held his head to one side, and especially the arrogant and crafty expression that suggested the past of a laborer fallen on good times, a man puffed up with influence and power.

In all, I had an uneasy feeling when I considered that this uncouth man shared a coach, and perhaps family ties, with the blonde and very young lady who had me enslaved. But the most disturbing thing about him was the strange brilliance of his eyes, and the hatred and choler I saw in them when the girl spoke the name of Captain Alatriste.

VII. THE PRADO RÚA

The next day was Sunday. It began in celebration but soon went downhill for Diego Alatriste and me, finally ending in tragedy. But let us not get ahead of ourselves.

The festivities centered around the *rúa*—the *rue*, the street, the *via*—which, in expectation of their official presentation at court and to the infanta, King Philip the Fourth ordered in honor of his illustrious guests. In those days, *hacer la rúa*—doing the *rúa*—was what the traditional *paseo* was called. All Madrid participated, on foot, on horseback, or in a carriage, whether along Calle Mayor, between Santa María de la Almudena and the steps of San Felipe and the Puerta del Sol, or whether continuing down to the gardens of the Duque de Lerma, the monastery of Saint Jerome—the Hieronymites—and the meadowland park, El Prado. Calle Mayor was the obligatory part of the *rúa*, from the center of the town to the Royal Palace, and it was also the location of silversmiths, jewelers, and elegant shops, which was why at dusk it was crowded with ladies' carriages and caballeros posturing before them. As for the *prado* of Saint Jerome, pleasant on sunny winter days and summer evenings, it was a green and leafy park with twenty-three fountains, many walled gardens, and a poplar-lined promenade where dignitaries in carriages and people strolling paused to exchange pleasantries. It was also a place for social meetings and trysts, perfect for furtive encounters, as well as the place where illustrious members of the court took their leisure. The one who best summed up the phenomenon of *hacer la rúa* was don Pedro Calderón de la Barca, several years later in one of his plays.

In early morning you will find me
At the church you often come to;
And as dusk falls, at the rúa,
Pray, may we rendezvous?
That night I shall drive through
The Prado, in the dark of my coach;
Then go on foot, in the dark of my cloak.
In this manner, I shall learn whether
With coach, mass, Prado, and my
Many hours on Calle Mayor
I have proven it is you I adore.

Nowhere, then, more suitable for our monarch, the fourth Philip—a romantic, as was proper for his young years—to propose as the site of the first official meeting between his sister, the infanta, and her gallant English suitor. Everything, naturally, was to occur within the limits of the decorum and protocol demanded by the Spanish court; rules so stringent that it was established long in advance what the royal family were to do every day and every hour of their lives. It is therefore not surprising that the unexpected visit of the illustrious aspiring brother-in-law-to-be should be seized upon by the monarch as a pretext for breaking from rigid royal etiquette to improvise parties and outings. Metaphorical shoulders were set to the wheel, and a *paseo* of carriages organized in which everyone who was anyone at court participated; the people were thereby witness to the kind of palace pomp that gratified their national pride, ceremonies the English undoubtedly found singular and astonishing.

Of course, when the future Charles the First inquired about the possibility of greeting his betrothed in person, exchanging even so much as a simple "Good evening," the Conde de Olivares and the other Spanish counselors looked gravely at one another before communicating to His Highness, with much diplomatic and political circumlocution, that he was reaching for a star. It was unthinkable that anyone, even a Prince of Wales, who had yet to be of-

ficially presented, should speak or approach the Infanta
doña María, or any other lady of the royal family. With
great discretion, they would see each other in passing, and
be grateful for that.

I myself was among the curious lining the street, and
I realized that the spectacle was the pinnacle of elegance
and refinement, with the cream of Madrid decked out in
their finery; but at the same time, because the visitors
were still officially incognito, everyone was acting nor-
mally, as if this were a day like any other. The prince,
Buckingham, the English ambassador, and the Conde de
Gondomar, our diplomat for London, took up a place at the
Guadalajara gate, in a closed coach—an *invisible* coach,
for express orders had been issued not to cheer or note its
presence—and from that vantage Charles watched as the
carriages carrying the royal family rolled by. In one of
them, beside our beautiful twenty-year-old queen, Isabel of
Bourbon, was the Infanta, doña María. At last the Prince
of Wales caught a glimpse of the blonde, pretty, circum-
spect girl she was in her youth. She was wearing a satiny
brocade gown and, around her wrist, the blue ribbon that
identified her to her suitor. Parading up and down Calle
Mayor and the Prado, the carriage passed before the
Englishmen three times that afternoon, and although the
prince caught only glimpses of blue eyes and a head of

golden hair adorned with plumes and precious stones, it was reported that he was immediately in thrall to our infanta.

And that must have been true, because he stayed on in Madrid for several months, seeking her hand as his wife while the king entertained him like a brother and the Conde de Olivares played him like a torero plays a bull, always with the greatest diplomacy. The advantage for Spain was that as long as there was hope of a marriage, the English stopped thumbing their noses at us while their pirates, their corsairs, their Dutch friends—the whole mutual ass-wiping lot—picked off our galleons returning from the Indies. So, we made merry as long as it lasted.

Ignoring the counsel of the Conde de Guadalmedina, Captain Alatriste did not raise a trail of dust getting out of town, or try to hide from anyone. I have recounted, in the previous chapter, how on the very morning that Madrid learned of the arrival of the Prince of Wales, the captain, as calm as you please, strolled back and forth in front of the House of Seven Chimneys. I even ran into him in the crowd on Calle Mayor in the midst of that festive Sunday *rúa*, staring pensively at the Englishmen's carriage. True, the brim of his hat was pulled low over his face, and the concealing folds of his cape were carefully arranged. After all, neither courtesy nor courage demands sharing one's secrets with the town crier.

Although the captain had not told me anything of his adventure, I was well aware that something had happened. The next night he had sent me to sleep at La Lebrijana's house, under the pretext that he was expecting guests in regard to a certain business dealing. But later I learned that he had spent the night awake, with two loaded pistols, a sword, and a dagger at his side. Nothing had happened, however, and with the light of dawn he lay down and slept the sleep of the just.

That was how I found him when I returned in the morning; the lamp had burned down, and was smoking, and he was sprawled across the bed, still in his wrinkled outergarments, his weapons within reach, breathing loudly and regularly through his mouth, an obstinate frown on his face.

Captain Alatriste was a fatalist. Perhaps his status as a former soldier—having fought in Flanders and the Mediterranean after running away from school to enlist as a page and drummer at the age of thirteen—was the reason he faced risk, misfortune, uncertainty, and the vagaries of a harsh and difficult life with the stoicism of one accustomed to expect nothing more. His nature was well defined in a description the French Maréchal de Grammont would later write of the Spanish: *"Courage comes quite naturally to them, as does patience in their labors and assurance in adversity.... Their gentleman soldiers rarely are amazed when things go badly, and they console themselves with the hope that soon their good fortune will return."* Or what a Frenchwoman, Madame d'Aulnoy, once said: *"You see them exposed to the affronts of weather and in extreme misery, yet despite all that, braver, haughtier, and prouder than they are amid opulence and prosperity."*

God knows that all this is true, and I, who knew such times, and some even worse that came later, give good witness to its truth. As for Diego Alatriste, he carried his hauteur and pride inside, and exhibited them only in his bullheaded silences. I have said already that unlike many braggarts who twirl their mustaches and talk loudly on street corners and at court, the captain was never heard to preen on the subject of his long military career. But sometimes, over a jug of wine, old comrades-in-arms dusted off stories about him, and I listened avidly. For to me in my young life, Diego Alatriste was the closest copy I had of the father who had fallen honorably in the wars of our lord and king. The captain was one of those small, tough, adamant men with whom Spain was always so well supplied, in good times and in bad, and to whom Calderón referred—and

may my master Alatriste, be he in glory, or elsewhere, forgive me that I so often quote don Pedro Calderón instead
of his beloved Lope—when he wrote:

> *. . . they stand foursquare,*
> *Stalwart, stolid, whether well or poorly paid.*
> *They have never known the vile shadow of fear,*
> *And though haughty, come to any man's aid.*
> *They are firm in the face of the worst danger,*
> *And rebel only when addressed in anger.*

I remember one episode that especially impressed me,
more than anything because of how clearly it showed
the nature of Captain Alatriste's character. Juan Vicuña,
the one who had been a sergeant in the horse guard of
our regiments during the disaster among the dunes at
Nieuwpoort—heavy-hearted the mother who had a son
there—several times described the defeat suffered by the
Spanish by laying out the battle lines on the table in the
Tavern of the Turk, using hunks of bread and jugs of wine
to demonstrate. He, my father, and Diego Alatriste had
been among the fortunate who saw the sun set on that ill-
fated day, something that cannot be said of five thousand
of his compatriots, including a hundred and fifty officers
and captains whose hides were tanned by the Dutch,
English, and French. Although those countries often fought

among themselves, they were quick enough to join together when it came to shoving it up our asses.

In Nieuwpoort, everything went their way: our field
commander, don Gaspar Zapena, was dead, and Admiral de
Aragón and other principal commanders captured. Our
troops were in disarray, and Juan Vicuña, who had lost all
his officers, and was himself wounded in one arm, which
he would lose to gangrene several weeks later, retired with
his decimated companies, along with the remaining foreign allied troops. And Vicuña recounted that when he
looked back for the last time, before putting on all speed
to retreat, he saw the veteran Tercio Viejo de Cartagena—
which was the company of my father and Alatriste—
attempting to quit a corpse-strewn battlefield through an
impenetrable wall of enemies, who with harquebuses and
muskets and artillery were making lace of the Spanish soldiers. There were dead, dying, and fleeing soldiers as far
as the eye could see, Vicuña said.

And in the midst of the disaster, under the blazing sun
reflecting dazzling light off the dunes, amid howling wind
and swirling sand that cloaked them in smoke and gunpowder, were the companies of the Tercio Viejo, bristling
with pikes, standing in square formation around flags
shredded by gunfire, and spitting musket balls in all four
directions. Amazingly, they were retreating at a measured
pace, without breaking ranks, dauntless, closing every

breach opened by an enemy artillery that did not dare come any closer to attack. On higher ground, the soldiers calmly consulted with their officers, and then resumed their march without missing a beat, terrifying even in defeat, as tightly organized and collected as if they were on parade, moving at the tempo set by the slow tattoo of their drums.

"The Cartagena *tercio* reached Nieuwpoort at nightfall," Vicuña concluded, using his only hand to move the jugs and last pieces of bread. "Always in step and unhurried, just seven hundred left of the fifteen hundred and fifty who had begun the battle. Lope Balbuena and Diego Alatriste were with them, black with gunpowder, thirsty, exhausted. They had been saved by not breaking formation, by keeping their heads in the midst of the general disaster. And do Your Mercies know what Diego replied when I ran to embrace him and congratulate him for still being alive? Well, he looked at me with those eyes of his, icy as the ball-freezing Holland canals, and said, 'We were too tired to run.'"

They did not come looking for him at night, as I expected, but in the late afternoon, and more or less officially. Someone knocked at the door, and when I opened it I saw the substantial figure of the head constable, Martín

Saldaña. His bailiffs were stationed on the stairs and in the courtyard—I counted half a dozen—and some had their swords unsheathed.

Saldaña came in alone, his belt sagging with the metal it held, and closed the door after himself, keeping his hat on and his sword in his baldric. Alatriste, in shirtsleeves, had jumped up and was waiting in the center of the room. As the constable entered, he took his hand from his dagger, which he had quickly grasped when he heard the knocking.

"Christ's blood, Diego, you are making this difficult for me," said Saldaña with bad humor, pretending not to see the two pistols on the table. "You should at least have left Madrid. Or moved to new lodgings."

"I was not expecting you."

"Yes, I can believe that I am not the one you were expecting." Saldaña finally looked at the pistols, walked a few steps into the room, took off his hat and set it over them, covering them. "Although you were expecting someone."

"And what am I supposed to have done?"

I was watching from the doorway to the other room, uneasy about this development. Saldaña looked at me a moment and then walked the other way. He had also been a friend of my father's, in Flanders.

"May I be struck by a thunderbolt if I know," he told

the captain. "My orders are to arrest you, or kill you if you resist."

"Of what am I accused?"

The lieutenant was evasive. He shrugged and said, "You are not accused of anything. Someone wants to speak with you."

"Who gave the orders?"

"That is none of your concern. Those are the orders I was given, and that is enough for me." Again he was looking at Alatriste with annoyance, as if chastising him for creating this mess. "May I know what is going on, Diego? You have no idea what you have stirred up."

Alatriste gave him a twisted smile, one with no trace of humor. "All I did was accept the assignment you recommended."

"Well, I curse the hour I did, 'pon my oath, I do!" Saldaña sighed a long, loud sigh. "By God, the men who employed you are not at all satisfied with how you carried it out."

"It was too dirty, Martín."

"Too dirty? And what does that matter? I cannot remember having done anything clean in the last thirty years. And I believe that may also be said of you."

"It was foul even by our standards."

"Say no more." Saldaña threw his hands up. "I do not want to know anything about anything. In these times knowing too much is worse than knowing too little." Again he looked at Alatriste, uncomfortable but resolute. "Are you going to come along quietly, or not?"

"What cards are you dealing me?"

Saldaña had little time to consider, but after a moment he came to a conclusion. "Very well. I can stay here while you test your luck with the men I have outside. They are not very skilled with their swords, but there are six of them. I doubt that even you can get to the street without a couple of souvenir slashes and likely a shot or two."

"And which way will we travel?"

"We go in a closed carriage, so you can forget about the route. You should have been away long before we came. You had more than enough time." The look Saldaña threw at the captain was heavy with reproach. "Damn my soul if I expected to find you here!"

"But where are you taking me?"

"I cannot tell you that. In truth, I have said much more than I should." I was still in the doorway, not moving, not talking, but the high constable noticed me for a second time. "Do you want me to look after the boy?"

"No, leave him here." Alatriste did not even turn toward me, absorbed in his thoughts. "La Lebrijana will see to him."

"As you wish. Are you coming?"

"Tell me *where*, Martín."

Saldaña shook his head, annoyed. "I have told you that I cannot."

"It would not be to the town prison, would it?"

Saldaña's silence was eloquent. Then on Captain Alatriste's face I saw that grimace that sometimes took the place of a smile.

"Do you have orders to kill me?" he asked serenely.

Again Saldaña shook his head. "No. I give you my word that my orders were to bring you back if you did not resist. Whether they will let you leave after I take you in is a different question. But by then you will no longer be my responsibility."

"If it weren't for the fuss it might make, they would have dispatched me right here." Alatriste pulled his finger across his throat, imitating the path of a knife. "They have sent you because they want official secrecy. Arrested, interrogated, and, they will say, set free afterward, and so on and so on. And in the meantime, who will know?"

Without hesitation, Saldaña nodded his agreement. "That is what I think," he said, matter-of-factly. "I am only surprised that they did not dream up charges; whether true or false, an accusation is the easiest thing in the world to fabricate. Maybe they are afraid you will speak out in public. If truth be known, my orders were to not exchange a single word with you. And they did not want me to list your name in my ledger of prisoners. God help you!"

"Let me bring a weapon, Martín."

The constable's jaw dropped open. "A *weapon?* . . . Not a chance," he said after a long pause.

Moving with extreme deliberation, the captain pulled out his slaughterer's knife and showed it to the constable. "Just this one."

"You have lost your senses. Do you take me for a blockhead?"

Alatriste shook his head no. "They want to kill me," he replied simply. "That is no surprise in my trade—it will happen sooner or later. But I never like to make things easy." Again that twisted smile flowered. "I swear that I will not use it against you."

Saldaña scratched his soldier's beard, which covered the long scar running from his mouth to his left ear. He had received it during the siege of Ostend, in the attacks on the redoubts of El Caballo and La Cortina, outside the walls. Among his companions on that day—and others—had been Diego Alatriste.

"Nor against any of my men," said Saldaña at last.

"On my oath."

The constable still hesitated. Then he turned his back, uttering blasphemous curses under his breath, as the captain slid the knife down the leg of a boot.

"Damn your eyes, Diego," said Saldaña, finally. "Let's get our asses out of here."

. . .

They left with no further conversation. The captain chose not to wear his cloak, to suggest he was defenseless, and Martín Saldaña agreed. He also allowed his old friend to wear a buffcoat over his doublet. "It will guard against the cold," he said, hiding a smile. As for me, I neither stayed at home nor went to Caridad la Lebrijana's. The minute they started down the stairs, without thinking twice I grabbed the pistols from the table and the sword hanging on the wall, and bundled them all up in the captain's cloak, then tucked them under my arm and ran after them.

There was very little day left in the sky of Madrid, barely a glow outlining rooftops and bell towers toward the Manzanares River and the Royal Palace. And so, at dusk, with shadows slowly creeping over the streets, I followed behind the closed carriage pulled by four mules, in which Martín Saldaña and his catchpoles were transporting the captain. They drove past the Jesuit school, down Calle Toledo, and into La Cebada plaza—undoubtedly to avoid busy streets—then turned toward the small hill of the Rastro fountain before again bearing right. They were almost at the outskirts of the city, very near the Toledo road, the slaughterhouse, and a site that had been a Moorish cemetery long before, but now, because of its bad reputation, was called the Portillo de las Ánimas. Given its macabre history and the gloomy hour, this Gate of Lost Souls was not the most comforting place in the world to be.

Night had definitely fallen when the carriage stopped before a deserted-looking house with two small windows and a large carriage courtyard that seemed better suited for horses than for anything else. I guessed that in the past it had been an inn for cattle traders. I stood at the corner, panting, hidden by a large carriage guard, with my bundle beneath my arm. I saw Alatriste, resigned and calm, get out of the carriage, surrounded by Saldaña and his bailiffs. They all went inside, and after a while I watched them come out without the captain, climb into the carriage, and leave. That disturbed me, for I did not know who else might be inside the house. I eliminated the idea of going any closer because I would run the certain risk of being caught.

And so, twitching with anxiety, but patient, "as every man-of-arms must be"—as I had heard Alatriste himself say—I squeezed back against the wall to blend into the darkness, and prepared to wait. I confess that I was cold and afraid. But I was the son of Lope Balboa, a soldier of the king who had died in Flanders. And I could not abandon my father's friend.

VIII. THE GATE OF LOST SOULS

It looked like a tribunal, and Diego Alatriste did not have the least doubt that it was. One of the masked men was absent, the corpulent one who had insisted that there be little blood. His companion, however—the man with the round head and coarse, thin hair—was there, wearing the same mask and sitting behind a long table on which there were a lighted candelabrum and writing materials: goose quills, paper, and inkwell. His hostile aspect and his attitude would have been the most disturbing thing in the world had it not been for someone more disturbing seated beside him. That person wore no mask, and his hands were bony serpents slithering from the sleeves of his habit: Fray Emilio Bocanegra.

There were no other chairs, so Captain Alatriste stood as he was questioned. It was, in fact, a standard interroga-

tion, a task with which the Dominican priest was well acquainted. It was obvious that he was furious, worlds away
from anything remotely related to Christian charity. The
wavering light from the candelabrum deepened his sunken,
badly shaved cheeks, and his eyes glittered with hatred as
they bore into Alatriste. His entire person, from the way in
which he asked questions to the least perceptible of his
movements, conveyed distilled menace; the captain glanced
around, looking for the rack on which, very soon, he would
be tortured. He was surprised that Saldaña had left with his
men, and that there were no guards in sight; it appeared
that only the masked man, the priest, and he were present.
He sensed something strange, a discordant note in all this.
Something was not as it should be. Or seemed to be.

The questioning by the Inquisitor and his companion,
who from time to time bent over the table to dip a feather
pen into the inkwell and jot down some observation, lasted
half an hour. In that time the captain had woven together
a fabric of places and circumstances, including why he
found himself there, alive, able to move his tongue and ar-
ticulate sounds, instead of sprawled on some dumping
ground with his throat cut like a dog.

What most concerned his interrogators was the question
of how much he had told, and to whom. Many questions
were directed toward the role of Guadalmedina on the
night of the adventure of the Englishmen, and especially

toward establishing how the count had become implicated, and how much he knew about the matter. The inquisitors also showed special interest in learning whether other parties had been informed, and the names of any who might have partial knowledge of the affair.

For his part, the captain kept his guard high, not admitting any act or divulging the identity of any person. He continued to maintain that Guadalmedina's intervention had been coincidental—although his questioners seemed to be convinced otherwise. Without a doubt, the captain reflected, someone inside the Alcázar Real had been informed of the comings and goings of the count that night, as well as the morning after the skirmish in the lane. But he held firm, sustaining that neither Álvaro de la Marca nor anyone else knew of his interview with the two masked men and the Dominican. For the most part, he answered in monosyllables, or by nodding or shaking his head. He was beginning to feel hot in the buffcoat, or perhaps it was only apprehension. He looked around the room, wondering which direction the executioners—who must be hidden somewhere—would come from, to take him prisoner and lead him in manacles to the anteroom of Hell.

There was a pause as the masked man took notes in a very deliberate and correct hand, that of a professional scribe, and the priest stared at Alatriste with that hypnotic, feverish gaze that would raise gooseflesh on the bravest of men. In the interim, the captain wondered when someone was going to ask him why he had blocked the Italian's sword. Apparently his personal motives in the matter were not worth a fart in a windstorm. At just that instant, as if he were able to read the captain's thoughts, Fray Emilio Bocanegra put out his hand and rested it on the dark table, with his waxy index finger pointed at the captain.

"What impels a man to desert the legions of God and pass into the iniquitous ranks of the heretics?"

It was nearly comic, thought Diego Alatriste, for the priest to qualify as God's legions the unit formed by him, the masked scribe, and that sinister Italian swordsman. In other circumstances, he would have burst out laughing, but this stage was not set for comedy. He choked back his laughter and, unflinching, met the Dominican's eyes, and then those of the scribe, who had stopped writing. The eyes glinting through the holes of his mask showed very little sympathy.

"I cannot say," said the captain. "It may have been because although the man was facing death, he asked for mercy for his companion, not himself."

The Inquisitor and the masked man exchanged incredulous looks.

"God save and protect us," muttered the priest. Eyes filled with fanaticism and scorn measured the captain.

I am a dead man, thought Alatriste, reading his sentence in those black and pitiless pupils. Whatever he did, whatever he said, his doom was written in that implacable stare and in the icy calm with which the man in the mask again put pen to paper. The life of Diego Alatriste y Tenorio, soldier of the Tercios Viejos in Flanders, hired swordsman in the Madrid of King Philip the Fourth, was worth only whatever those two men still wanted to learn. As one could deduce from the turn the conversation was taking, that was very little indeed.

"Your companion that night"—the scribe spoke without interrupting his writing, and his surly tone sounded a death knell for the captain—"did not seem to have as many scruples as you."

"I give faith to that," the captain admitted. "He seemed even to be enjoying it."

The writer's quill paused a moment in midair, as he flashed a look of irony toward the captain. "How wicked of him. And you?"

"I do not enjoy killing. For me, taking a life is a business, not a pleasure."

"Yes, so we noted." The man dipped the quill into the inkwell and turned back to his task. "And next, I suppose, we shall learn that you are a man given to Christian charity."

"You err, Your Mercy," the captain responded serenely. "I am known to be a man more inclined toward the sword than toward sentiment."

"That is why you were recommended to us as a man of the sword. To our misfortune."

"But in truth, it is so. Fortune has reduced me to this sad estate. I have been a soldier all my life, and there are certain things one cannot avoid."

The Dominican, who had been as quiet as the Sphinx during this exchange, sat straight up and leaned across the table toward Alatriste as if he would obliterate him on the spot. That instant.

"Avoid? You soldiers are offal," he declared with infinite repugnance. "Rabble . . . blaspheming, looting, wallowing with women. What infernal 'sentiment' do you refer to? Taking a life is as easy as breathing to you."

The captain received the reproof in silence, and only when the priest had finished did he shrug.

"You are undoubtedly right," he said. "But some things are difficult to explain. I was going to kill that Englishman. And I would have, had he defended himself or sought mercy for himself. But when he pled for mercy, it was as I told you, he pled for the other man."

The round-headed man again paused in his writing. "Did they, by any chance, reveal their identity to you?"

"No, although they could have, and perhaps saved themselves. I was a soldier for nearly thirty years. I have killed, and I have done things for which my soul will be damned through eternity. But I know how to appreciate the gesture of a courageous man. And heretics or not, those men were courageous."

"You give that much importance to courage?"

"There are times when courage is all that is left," the captain said with utter simplicity. "Especially in times like these, when even flags and the name of God are used to strike deals."

If he had expected a reply, there was none. The masked man did nothing but continue to stare at him. "By now, of course, you have learned who those two Englishmen are."

Alatriste said nothing, but finally allowed a weak sigh to escape. "Would you believe me if I denied it? Since yesterday, all of Madrid has known." He looked at the Dominican and then the masked man with an expression that was easy to read. "And I am happy not to have that on my conscience."

The scribe made a brusque movement, as if attempting to shake off the thing Diego Alatriste had not wanted to be responsible for. "You bore us with your inopportune conscience, *Captain.*"

This was the first time he had used that form of address. It was consciously ironic, and Alatriste frowned, not pleased.

"It matters little whether I bore you or not," he replied. "I do not like to murder princes without knowing who they are." Irritated, he twisted his mustache. "Or to be deceived and manipulated."

"And you feel no curiosity," intervened the priest, who had been listening closely, "as to why just men had determined to procure those deaths? Or prevent evil men from usurping the good faith of our lord and king, and from taking an infanta of Spain to the land of heretics as a hostage?"

Alatriste slowly shook his head. "No, I am not curious. Please consider, Your Mercies, that I have not even attempted to find out who this gentleman is who covers his face with a mask." Alatriste looked at his questioners with mocking, insolent seriousness. "Nor the identity of the one who, before he left the other night, insisted that I should merely frighten Masters John and Thomas Smith, take their letters and documents, but spare their lives."

For a moment the Dominican and his companion said nothing. They seemed to be thinking. It was the latter who finally spoke, staring at his ink-stained fingernails.

"Perhaps you suspect who that other caballero might be?"

"'Sblood! I suspect nothing. I find myself involved in something that is too rich for my fancy, and I regret it. Now all I hope to do is to leave with my head attached to my body."

"Too late," said the priest, in a tone so low and menacing that it reminded the captain of the hissing of a snake.

"Returning to our two Englishmen," the masked man put in. "You will recall that after the other caballero left, you received different instructions from the holy father and from me."

"I remember. But I also remember that you yourself seemed to show special deference to that 'other caballero,' and that you did not reveal your orders until he was gone and the . . . holy father"—Alatriste looked out of the corner of his eye at the Inquisitor: remote, impassive, as if all this had nothing to do with him—"had stepped from behind the tapestry. That too may have influenced my decision regarding the lives of the Englishmen."

"You accepted good money not to respect them."

"True." The captain put his hand to his belt. "And here it is."

The gold coins rolled across the table and lay gleaming in the light of the candles. Fray Emilio Bocanegra did not even look at them, as though they were cursed. But the masked man reached for them and counted them one by one, stacking them into two small piles beside the inkwell.

"You are four doubloons short," he said.

"Yes. That is payment for my trouble. And for having been taken for an imbecile."

The Dominican exploded with a flash of choler. "You are a traitor, and totally untrustworthy," he said, contempt vibrating in his voice. "With your untimely attack of scruples, you have favored the enemies of God and of Spain. All this will be purged from you, I promise, in the cauldrons of Hell, but before that you will pay dearly here on earth. With your mortal flesh." The word "mortal" sounded even more terrifying coming from those icy, clenched lips. "You have seen too much, you have heard too much, you have made too many errors. Your life, Captain Alatriste, is worth nothing. You are a cadaver that—through some strange chance—is still walking and talking."

As the Dominican made that fearsome threat, the masked man was sprinkling powder on the sheet before him, to dry the ink. Then he folded it and put it into a pocket, and as he did, Alatriste again glimpsed the tip of the red cross of Calatrava beneath his black cloak. He also observed that the hands with the blackened nails collected the coins, apparently forgetting that part of them had come from the purse of the Dominican.

"You may go," the priest said to Alatriste, looking at him as if he had just remembered he was there.

The captain looked back at him with surprise. "I am free?"

"In a manner of speaking," added Fray Emilio Bocanegra, with a smile equivalent to excommunication. "You go with the weight of your treachery and our curses around your neck."

"That will not be heavy." Alatriste turned from one to the other, incredulous. "Is it true that I may leave? Now?"

"That is what we said. The wrath of God will know where to find you."

"The wrath of God does not worry me tonight. But Your Mercies . . ."

The Dominican and the scribe were on their feet. "We have concluded," said the former.

Alatriste studied their faces. The candlelight from below cast ominous shadows.

"I find that difficult to believe," Alatriste concluded. "After you had me brought here."

"That," said the masked man as a last word, "no longer has anything to do with us."

They walked out, taking the candelabrum with them, and the last thing Diego Alatriste saw was the terrible gaze the Dominican threw his way before crossing his arms and thrusting his hands into the sleeves of his habit. The two men faded away like shadows. Instinctively, the captain reached for the grip of the sword that was not at his waist.

"A pox on them! Where is the trap in all this?"

His question was pointless, echoing through the empty room. There was no answer. As he strode toward the door, he remembered the slaughterer's knife he carried in his bootleg. He bent down and pulled it out, gripping it firmly, awaiting the attack of the executioners who, he was sure, were waiting for him.

But none came. He was inexplicably alone in the room dimly illuminated by the rectangle of moonlight falling through the window.

I do not know how long I waited outside, blending into the darkness, motionless behind the carriage guard on the corner post. I clutched the captain's cape and weapons closer, to borrow a little warmth from them—I was wearing only my doublet and hose when I ran after the coach of Martín Saldaña and his catchpoles—and stood there a long while, clenching my teeth to keep them from chattering. Finally, when neither the captain nor anyone else came out of the house, I began to be concerned. I could not believe that Saldaña had murdered my master, but in that city at that time, anything was possible. The idea truly alarmed me. When I looked closely I thought I could see a sliver of light escaping through one of the windows, as if someone were inside with a lamp, but from where I stood it was impossible to verify. I decided, despite the danger, to try to get near enough to peek inside.

I was about to step into the open, when, in one of those strokes of fortune to which we sometimes owe our lives, I caught a glimpse of movement some distance away, in the entry to a neighboring house. It was only a flicker, but a shadow had moved as the shadows of motionless objects do when they become animate. Surprised, I swallowed my impatience and stood there, undecided, keeping my eyes glued to the spot. After a while, it moved again, and at that same moment, from across the small plaza I heard a soft whistle that sounded like a signal: a little tune, something like *ti-ri-tu, ta-ta*. When I heard that, the blood froze in my veins.

There must be at least two, I decided, after scrutinizing the shadows that covered the Gate of Lost Souls. One of them was hiding in the nearest entryway; that was the first shadow that had moved. The second, the one that had whistled, was farther away, covering the angle of the plaza that led to the wall of the slaughterhouse. There were three ways out, so for a while I concentrated on the third. Finally, when the clouds parted to reveal a crescent moon, I was rewarded: I made out a third dark shape, silhouetted against the moonlight.

The plan was clear, and boded ill for the captain, but I had no way to run the thirty steps to the house without being seen. I pondered these developments, and sat down and unrolled the cape, then placed one of the pistols on my knees. Its use was forbidden by edict of our lord and king, and I was well aware that if the law found me with them, my young bones would end up in a galley, and my youth would not excuse me. But, upon my word as a Basque, at that moment I did not give a fig. So, as I had watched the captain do so many times, I felt to see that the flint stone was in place, and trying to muffle the click with the cape, I pulled back the hammer to cock the pistol for firing. That one I stuck between my doublet and my shirt. I primed the second pistol, and waited with it in one hand and the captain's sword in the other. I put the now empty cape around my shoulders, and thus equipped, I continued my vigil.

I did not have long to wait. A light shone briefly in the enormous entry to the house, then was extinguished. I heard a carriage and turned to see it approaching from one of the exits of the small plaza. Along with it, I made out a black silhouette that entered the courtyard and for a brief instant consulted with two dark figures that had emerged from the house. The first shadow returned to its corner, and the other figures climbed into the carriage. As it started off, with its black mules and funereal coachman, it passed so close that it nearly brushed against me, then it rolled off into the darkness.

I did not have long to reflect upon the mysterious carriage. The sound of the mules' hooves was still echoing across the plaza when from the spot where the black silhouette was posted came another whistle, again that *ti-ri-tu, ta-ta,* and from the nearest corner the unmistakable sound of a sword being slowly drawn from its scabbard. Desperately, I prayed to God to part the clouds once more, and allow me to see. But it is a long way from thinking about the horse to saddling it. Our Supreme Maker must have been busy with other duties, because the clouds stayed where they were. I began to feel light-headed; everything around me was whirling. So I shed the cape and stood, meaning to run more quickly to the place where things were going to happen. That was when I saw Captain Alatriste come out into the courtyard.

Then everything happened with extraordinary speed. The shadow closest to me moved from its hiding place, starting toward Diego Alatriste at almost the same time I did. I held my breath as I followed it: one, two, three steps. At just that moment, God chose to shed his light on me, and parted the clouds. In the pale glow of the crescent moon I could clearly make out the back of a heavyset man moving forward with naked steel in his hand. I also saw the other two starting from their corners of the plaza. And as I held the captain's sword in my left hand and raised my right, armed with the pistol, I saw Diego Alatriste stop in the middle of the plaza, and caught the glint from his useless knife.

I took two steps more, and now the barrel of the pistol was nearly prodding the back of the man in front of me . . . but he heard my footsteps and whirled about. I had time to see his face before I pulled the trigger and the pistol went off. The flash of the shot lighted features distorted with surprise. The roar of the gunpowder thundered through the Gate of Lost Souls.

The rest happened even more rapidly. I yelled, or thought I did, partly to alert the captain, and partly because of the terrible pain from the recoil of the weapon; it felt as if my arm had been torn from its socket. But the captain had more warning than he needed from the shot, and when I threw him his sword, over the shoulder of the man in front of me—or over the place where the man in front of me had been—he was already running toward it. He danced aside to avoid being hit, and picked it up the moment it touched the ground. Then, once again, the moon hid behind the clouds. I dropped the discharged pistol, pulled the other from my doublet, and turned toward the two shadows closing in on the captain.

I aimed, holding the pistol with both hands. But I was trembling so hard that the second shot went wild, and this time the recoil knocked me backward to the ground. As I fell, my eyes dazzled by the flash, I had a second's glimpse of two men with swords and daggers, and of Captain Alatriste, sword flashing, battling like a demon.

Diego Alatriste had seen them coming toward him before the first pistol shot. The moment he stepped outside he was watching for something of the sort, and he knew how futile it would be to try to save his hide with his ridiculous knife. The blast of the pistol had shocked him as much as it had the others, and for an instant he had thought he was the target. Then he heard my yell, and still not understanding what the devil I was doing there at such a late hour, he saw his sword flying toward him as if it had fallen from the skies. In the blink of an eye he had it in his hand, just in time to confront two furious, deadly blades.

It was the flash from the second shot that allowed him, once the ball went whizzing by between his attackers and himself, to size up the situation and prepare. Now he knew that one was on his left and the other straight ahead of him, forming an angle of approximately ninety degrees.

The role of the one was to keep him engaged as the other plunged a knife into his ribs or belly from the side.

Alatriste had found himself in similar situations before; it was not an easy task to combat one while protecting himself from another with only a short knife. His defense was to slash a wide swath from right to left, to cut into their space, although to protect his vulnerable left side he was forced to swing more to the left than to the right. The two attackers met move with move, so that after a dozen feints and thrusts they had traced a complete circle around him. Two oblique stabs had glanced off his buffcoat. The *cling, clang* of the Toledo blades sounded the length and breadth of the plaza, and I have no doubt that had the place been more inhabited, between that noise and my pistol shots the windows would have been filled with observers.

Then Fate, which like the winds of war, favors those who keep a clear head, came to the aid of Diego Alatriste. It was God's will that one of his thrusts went through the quillons of the sword guard and cut either the fingers or the wrist of the adversary at his left, who when he felt the wound, stepped back two paces with a "For the love of . . ." By the time his opponent regrouped, Alatriste had already delivered three two-handed slashes, like three lightning bolts, against the other opponent, who had lost his balance and been forced by the violence of the attack to retreat.

That was all the captain needed to get his feet firmly set, and when the one who had been wounded on the hand advanced, the captain dropped the knife in his left hand, protected his face with his open palm, and lunging forward, thrust a good fourth of his blade into his opponent's chest. His victim's momentum did the rest: the sword drove through to the guard. The man cried out, *"Jesús!"* and dropped his sword, which clanged to the ground behind the captain.

The second swordsman, already on the attack, pulled up short. Alatriste leaped backward to pull his sword free of the first man—who had dropped to the ground like a sack of meal—and turned to face his remaining enemy, panting to catch his breath. The clouds had parted just enough to see, in the moonlight . . . the Italian.

"We are even now," said the captain, gasping for air.

"Delighted to hear that," the Italian replied, white teeth flashing in his dark face. The words were not yet out of his mouth when he made a quick, low thrust, as visible, and invisible, as the strike of an asp. The captain, who had studied the Italian carefully on the night of the attack on the two Englishmen, was waiting. He shifted to one side, and put out his left hand to parry the thrust, and the enemy sword plunged into thin air—although, as the captain stepped back, he became aware that he had a dagger cut across the back of his hand. Confident that the Italian had not severed a tendon, he reached to the left with his right arm, hand high and sword tip pointing down, parrying with a sharp *ting!* a second thrust, as surprising and skillful as the first. The Italian retreated one step, and again the two men stood facing each other, breathing noisily. Fatigue was beginning to affect both. The captain moved the fingers of his wounded hand, finding, to his relief, that they responded: the tendons were not cut. He felt blood, dripping warm and slow down his fingers.

"Can we not come to some agreement?" Alatriste asked.

The Italian stood in silence a moment. Then shook his head. "No," he said. "You went too far the other night." His throaty voice sounded tired. The captain could imagine that, like him, the Italian had had his fill.

"So now?"

"Now it is your head or mine."

A new silence. Alatriste's erstwhile accomplice made a slight move, and Alatriste responded, without relaxing his guard. Very slowly they circled, each taking the other's measure. Beneath the buffcoat, the captain could feel his shirt soaked in sweat.

"Will you tell me your name?"

"It has no bearing on this."

"You hide it, then—that is the sign of a scoundrel."

Alatriste heard the Italian's harsh laugh. "Perhaps. Yet

I am a live scoundrel, and you, Captain Alatriste, are a dead man."

"Not this night."

His adversary seemed to be taking stock. He glanced toward the inert body of his henchman. Then he looked at me, still on the ground beside the third of the figures who had been lurking in the plaza, and who was now stirring weakly. He must have been badly wounded by my pistol shot, for we could hear him moaning and asking for confession.

"No," concluded the Italian. "I believe you are right. This is not the night."

He seemed to be readying himself to leave, but as I watched, I saw him flip the dagger in his left hand from grip to blade. Then, all in the same movement, he flung it toward the captain, who somehow miraculously dodged it.

"Underhanded dog!" grunted Alatriste.

"Well, by God," the other responded. "You surely didn't think I would ask your permission."

Again the two swordsmen stood studying each other. The Italian ended that with a twirl of his blade, Alatriste responded with another, and again each cautiously raised his sword, and steel brushed steel with a faint metallic *ching*, before they lowered their swords again.

"Devil take it," the Italian sighed hoarsely. "There is no

end to this." He began to back away from the captain, very slowly, his sword held horizontally between them. Only when he was safely away, almost at the corner post, did he turn his back.

"Incidentally," he called as he was fading into the shadows, "the name is Gualterio Malatesta. Did you hear? And I come from Palermo. I want that burned into your brain when I kill you!"

The man I had shot was still whimpering for confession. His shoulder was shattered, and splinters of his clavicle were protruding from the wound. Very soon, the Devil would be well served.

Diego Alatriste gave him a quick, impersonal look, went through his purse, as he had earlier with the dead man's, and then came over and knelt beside me. He did not thank me, or say any of the things one might expect would be said when a thirteen-year-old boy has saved a man's life. He simply asked if I was all right, and when I replied that I was, he tucked his sword beneath one arm and, putting the other around my shoulders, helped me to my feet. His mustache brushed my cheek for an instant, and I saw that his eyes, paler than ever in the light of the moon, were observing me with strange intensity, as if he were seeing me for the first time.

The dying man moaned again, again pleading for confession. The captain turned back, and I could see him thinking.

"Run over to San Andrés," he said finally, "and fetch a priest for this miserable fellow."

I stared at him, hesitating; it seemed to me that I had glimpsed that bitter, ill-humored grimace on his lips.

"His name is Ordóñez," he added. "I recognize him from Flanders."

Then he picked up the pistols and started off. Before I obeyed his orders, I went back to the carriage guard on the corner to look for his cape, then ran after him and handed it to him. He tossed it over one shoulder and lightly touched my cheek—with a show of affection unusual in him. And he kept looking at me with the same expression he had had when he asked if I was all right. Half embarrassed, half proud, I felt a drop of blood from his wounded hand drip onto my face.

IX. THE STEPS OF SAN FELIPE

A few days of calm followed that sleepless night. But as Diego Alatriste continued to refuse to leave the city, or hide, we lived in a perpetual state of alert; we might as well have been in a campaign. Staying alive, I discovered, can be much more tiring than letting oneself be killed, and requires all five senses. The captain slept more during the day than he did at night, and at the least sound—a cat on the roof, or the creak of wood on the stairs—I would awaken in my bed to see him in his nightshirt, sitting up in his, with the *vizcaína* or a pistol in his hand.

After the skirmish at the Gate of Lost Souls, he had tried to send me back to my mother for a while, or to the house of a friend. I told him that I had no intention of abandoning our camp, that his fate was mine, and that if I had been capable of getting off two pistol shots, I could fire off another twenty if the occasion demanded. A position I reinforced by expressing my determination to run away from any place he might send me. I do not know whether Alatriste was grateful for my decision, for I have told you that he was not a man given to revealing his feelings. But at least I had made my point. He shrugged and did not bring up the matter again.

In fact, the next day I found a fine dagger on my pillow, recently purchased on Calle de los Espaderos: damascened handle, steel cross-guard, and a long, finely tempered blade, slim and double-edged. It was one of those daggers our grandfathers called a *misericordia,* for it was used to put caballeros fallen in battle out of their misery. That was the first weapon I ever possessed, and I kept it, with great fondness, for twenty years, until one day in Rocroi I had to leave it buried between the fastenings of a Frenchman's corselet. Which is actually not a bad end for a fine dagger like that one.

All the time that we were sleeping with one eye open, and jumping at our own shadows, Madrid was ablaze with celebrations occasioned by the visit of the Prince of Wales, an event that was by now official. There were days of cavalcades, soirées in the Alcázar Real, banquets, receptions, and masked balls, all topped off with a festival of "bulls and canes" in the Plaza Mayor that I remember as one of the most outstanding spectacles of its kind ever seen in our Madrid of the Austrias. The finest caballeros in the whole city—among them our young king—took part, wielding lances or pikes and pitting themselves against Jarama bulls in a glorious display of grace and courage. This fiesta of the *corrida* was, as it continues to be today, the favorite celebration of the people of Madrid—and of no few other places in Spain. The king himself, and our beautiful Queen Isabel—though a daughter of the great Henri IV, the Béarnais, and through him Elizabeth of France—were very fond of them. My lord and king, the fourth Philip, was known to be an elegant horseman and a fine shot, an aficionado of the hunt and of horses—once, in a single day, killing three wild boars by his own hand but losing a fine mount in the process. His sporting skills were immortalized in the paintings of don Diego Velázquez, as well as in poems by many authors and poets such as Lope de Vega or Francisco de Quevedo. These lines by don Pedro Calderón de la Barca are from his popular play *La banda y la flor*:

> *Shall I tell what gallant horseman*
> *Decked out in high boots and spurs,*
> *Arms at a pleasing angle, the hand*
> *Held low to rein in his steed,*
> *Cape neatly arranged, back*
> *Ramrod-straight, eyes alert,*

Trotted elegantly through the streets
Beside the carriage of the queen?

I have already said elsewhere that in his eighteenth or twentieth year, Philip was—and would be for many years—congenial, fond of the ladies, elegant, and beloved of his people. Ah, our good, mistreated Spanish people, who always considered their kings to be the most just and magnanimous on earth, even when their power was on the decline; even though the reign of the previous king, Philip the Third, had been brief, but with time enough to be calamitous left in the hands of an incompetent and venal favorite; and even though our young monarch, a consummate horseman, if lethargic and incapable in affairs of government, was at the mercy of the accomplishments and disasters—and there were many more of the latter—of the Conde, and later Duque, de Olivares.

The Spanish people—or at least what is left of them—have changed a great deal since then. Their pride and admiration for their king was followed by scorn; enthusiasm by acerbic criticism; dreams of greatness by deep depression and general pessimism.

I well remember—and I believe this happened during the festival of the bulls honoring the Prince of Wales, or perhaps a later one—that one of the beasts was so fierce that it could not be hamstrung or slowed. No one—not even the Spanish, Burgundian, and German guards ornamenting the plaza—dared go near it. Then, from the balcony of the Casa de la Panadería, our good King Philip, calm as you please, asked one of the guards for his harquebus. Without losing a whit of royal composure or making any grandiose gestures, he casually took the gun, went down to the plaza, threw his cape over his shoulder, confidently requested his hat, and aimed so true that lifting the weapon, firing it, and dropping the bull were all one and the same motion.

The public exploded in applause and cheers, and for months the feat was celebrated in both prose and verse. Calderón, Hurtado de Mendoza, Alarcón, Vélez de Guevara, Rojas, Saavedra Fajardo, and don Francisco de Quevedo himself—everyone at court capable of dipping a quill into an inkwell—invoked the Muses to immortalize the act and adulate the monarch, comparing him now with Jupiter sending down his bolt of lightning, now with Theseus slaying the bull at Marathon. I remember that don Francisco's sonnet began with a clever wordplay, in which he combined the continent of Europe and the mythic figure of Europa.

In leaving dead the rapist of Europa,
Of whom you are lord, as monarch of Spain . . .

And the great Lope, addressing his lines to the charging bull eliminated by the royal hand, wrote:

Both blessing and tragedy was your death,
For, though life gave you no reason to live,
Greatness came with your dying breath.

This even though at that point in his life, Lope did not need to fawn on anyone. I tell these things that Your Mercies may see what Spain is, and what we Spaniards are like, how our good and gentle people have always been abused, and how easy, because of our generous impulses, it is to win us over, and push us to the brink of the abyss out of meanness or incompetence, when we have always deserved better. Had Philip IV commanded the glorious *tercios* of old, had he retaken Holland, conquered Louis XIII of France and his minister Richelieu, cleared the Atlantic of pirates and the Mediterranean of Turks, invaded England and raised the cross of Saint Andrew at the Tower of London and before the Sublime Porte, he could not have awakened as much enthusiasm among his subjects as he did with his élan in killing a bull.

How different from that other Philip IV, the widower with dead, weak, or degenerate sons, whom I myself would have to escort—along with his retinue—more than thirty years later across a deserted Spain devastated by wars, hunger, and misery, tepidly cheered by the few miserable peasants with energy enough to gather along the roadside. Bereaved, aged, head bowed, traveling to the border at the Bidassoa River to undergo the humiliation of delivering his daughter in marriage to a French king, and in so doing, sign the death certificate of that unhappy Spain he had led to disaster, squandering the gold and silver from America in vain frivolities, in enriching officials, clergy, nobles, and corrupt favorites, and in filling the battlefields of Europe with the graves of courageous men.

But it is not my wish to skip over years or events. The time I am writing about was still many years from such a dismal future, and Madrid still the capital of the Spains and the world. Those days, like the weeks that followed, and the months the engagement between our Infanta María and the Prince of Wales lasted, both town and court spent in entertainments of every nature. The most beautiful ladies and most genteel caballeros outdid themselves to fête the royal family and their illustrious guest during *rúas* along Calle Mayor and into El Prado park, and in elegant *paseos* through the gardens of the Alcázar, past the Acero fountain, and into the pine forests of the Casa de Campo, the royal country estate.

The strictest rules of etiquette and decorum between

the courting pair were, naturally, respected; they were never alone for a moment, always—to the despair of the impetuous young swain—watched over by a swarm of majordomos and duennas. Indifferent to the quiet diplomatic tussles unleashed in the chancelleries—for or against the union—the nobility and the common people of Madrid tried to outdo each other in their homage to the heir to the English throne, and to the compatriots joining him at court. Tittle-tattle flew on street corners and in drawing rooms: the infanta was learning the English tongue, and Charles himself was studying Catholic doctrine with theologians, with the goal of embracing the true faith. Nothing was further from reality in regard to the latter, as would be proved later. But at the moment, and in such a climate of goodwill, whispers about the charm, consideration, and good looks of the young heir merely added to his popularity.

This reputation would later serve to offset the caprices and insolence of Buckingham, who, as he gained more confidence—he had just been named a duke by his king, James—and as both he and Charles came to realize that the negotiations for the marriage would be arduous and long, was revealing all the earmarks of a spoiled, bad-mannered, arrogant young man. Something that serious Spanish hidalgos found difficult to tolerate, especially in regard to three matters that were sacred at the time: protocol, religion, and women. Buckingham's uncouth behavior reached such an extreme that, on more than one occasion, only the hospitality and good breeding of our caballeros prevented their slapping the Englishman across the face with a glove in answer to some insolence or other, which would have led to settling the question with seconds and swords, at dawn, in El Prado park or at the Puerta de la Vega. As for the Conde de Olivares, his relationship with Buckingham went from bad to worse after the first days of obligatory political courtesy, and in the long run, after the engagement was dissolved, there were unfortunate consequences for Spanish interests.

Now that years have gone by, I wonder whether it would not have been better had Diego Alatriste skewered the Englishman that famous night, despite his scruples and no matter how noble the accursed heretic had showed himself to be. But who could have known? At any rate, our friend Buckingham would get his comeuppance in his own country, when some years later a Puritan lieutenant named Felton—upholding, they say, the honor of a certain Milady de Winter—gave him what he deserved: more stabs in the gut than a missal has prayers.

Well, to sum up: Those particulars are plentiful in the annals of the epoch. I recommend them to the reader interested in more details, for they have no direct relation to the thread of this story. I shall say only, in regard to Captain Alatriste and myself, that we neither participated in the festivities, to which it had been thought best not to invite us, nor had any desire to do so, should the invitation have been given. The days after the altercation at the Gate of Lost Souls went by, as I have said, without incident, undoubtedly because the puppeteer pulling the strings was too occupied with the public comings and goings of Charles of Wales to tend to such small details—and when I speak of small details, I am referring to the captain and me.

We were aware, however, that sooner or later the bill would be delivered, and it would not be inconsequential. After all, however cloudy it may be, the shadow is always sewn to one's feet. No one can escape his own shadow.

This is not the first time I have referred to the *mentideros* devoted to gossip—meeting places for the idle and centers for all the news, rumors, and whispers that traveled around Madrid. There were three main *mentideros*—San Felipe, Losas de Palacio, and Representantes—and among these, the one in front of the Augustinian church of San Felipe, between Correos, Mayor, and Esparteros, was the most crowded. The steps were at the entrance to the church, and because the building was not on a level with Calle Mayor, they were higher than the street, leaving room beneath for a row of small shops, cubbyholes where toys, guitars, and trinkets were sold. Their roofs, in turn, formed an area paved with large flat stones: a kind of elevated promenade protected with railings. From that theater box one had a wonderful view of people and carriages passing by, and could comfortably stroll from one group to another.

San Felipe was the liveliest, noisiest, and most popular spot in Madrid. Its proximity to the Estafeta, the building that housed the royal mails, where letters and notices from the rest of Spain, indeed, the entire world, were received, as well as its location overlooking the principal street of the city, made it an ideal site for the great public party in which opinions and gossip were exchanged, soldiers preened, clergy spread tales, thieves pilfered purses, and poets aired their talent and wit. Lope, don Francisco de Quevedo, and the Mexican Alarcón, among others, were regulars. Any news, rumor, or lie that originated there rolled like a ball gaining momentum; nothing escaped the tongues that knew everything, that shredded the reputations of everyone from king to lowest of low.

Many years later, Agustín Moreto mentioned San Felipe in one of his plays, when a countryman and a gallant military man meet:

> "*I see these steps are something you cannot leave!*"
> "*These knowing stones have me bewitched,*

My friends and I invariably leave enriched,
For nowhere in all the world have I
Encountered such a fertile ground for lies."

Even the great don Miguel de Cervantes, may he sit forever at the right hand of God, wrote in his *Voyage to Parnassus*:

Farewell, San Felipe, the grand paseo,
Where if the Turk descends or the English menace,
I read of it in the gazette of Venice.

I quote these lines that Your Mercies may see just how famous the place was. In its cliques, the state of affairs in Flanders, Italy, and the Indies were argued with the gravity of a meeting of the Council of Castile. Jokes and witticisms were traded; the honor of ladies, actresses, and cuckolded husbands was besmirched; foul obscenities were directed toward the Conde de Olivares; and the amorous adventures of the king spread in whispers from ear to ear.

It was, all told, a most pleasant and sparkling place, a font of wit, news, and wicked tongues that drew a gathering every morning about eleven. That lasted until the pealing of the church bell one hour after the noontime Angelus had stirred people in the crowd to remove their hats, stand respectfully, then drift away, leaving the field to the beggars, students, slatterns, and ragamuffins waiting for the soup from the charitable Augustinians. The steps came back to life in the evening, at the hour of the *rúa* on Calle Mayor, where rumor-mongers and tale-bearers could watch the passing parade of coaches: fine ladies; women of questionable reputation who gave themselves the airs of ladies; and "schoolgirls" from nearby brothels—there was a notorious one, actually, right across the street—all of them a source of conversation, flirtation, and jest. That lasted until the call to evening prayer, when, after praying with hat in hand, people in the crowd again dispersed until the following day, each to his own home—and God to all of theirs.

I stated earlier that don Francisco de Quevedo frequented the steps of San Felipe; and in many of his *paseos* he was accompanied by such friends as Licenciado Calzas, Juan Vicuña, or Captain Alatriste. His fondness for my master was based, among other factors, in practicality. The poet was always involved in quarrels rooted in jealousy and exchanging obscenities with various rivals—something very typical in that day, and in all epochs of this benighted country of ours, with its Cains, calumny, trickery, and envy, where words offended, even maimed, as surely as or more surely than the sword. Some, like Luis de Góngora and Juan Ruiz de Alarcón, were always belittling each other, and not merely for what they wrote.

Góngora, for example, said of Francisco de Quevedo:

Muse that babbles inanities
Can earn no ducats or hope to inspire;
His fingers know better to rob my purse
Than pluck at that unmelodious lyre.

And the next day it would be the other way around. Don Francisco would counterattack with his heaviest artillery:

This Góngora, who blasts a mighty fart,
This acme of vice and fanfaronade,
This asshole, in flesh and also in art,
Is a man even buggerers seek to evade.

And along with these lines, he fired off other verses, as famous as they were ferocious, that flew from one end of the city to another, portraying Góngora as filthy in both body and lineage.

In person—and breeding—so far from clean,
In fact, so precisely the opposite,
That never, as far as I have heard,
Did a word leave his mouth that wasn't shit.

Such sweet sentiments. He also turned out cruel lines aimed at poor Ruiz de Alarcón, whose physical impediment—a hunchback—he loved to deride with pitiless wit.

Sacks of meal on back and chest.
Who's the one with those effects?
Alarconvex!

Such verses circulated anonymously, in theory; but everyone knew perfectly well who had composed them— and with the worst intentions in the world. Naturally, other poets did not hold back: sonnets and *décimas* flew back and forth. To sharpen his claws, don Francisco would read his aloud in the *mentideros*, attacking and counterattacking, his pen dipped in the most corrosive bile. And if he wasn't defiling Góngora or Alarcón, it might be anyone at all; for on those days when the poet woke up spewing vitriol, he fired randomly at anyone who moved.

In regard to those horns you are forced to wear,
Don Whoever You Be, who put them there?
Your unfaithful wife, and if they are trimmed
She will help you grow them all over again!

Lines of that nature. So many that even though Quevedo was courageous, and skillful with the sword, having a man like Diego Alatriste beside him when he strolled among prospective adversaries was comforting for him. And it happened that one morning when don Francisco was out with Captain Alatriste, Señor Whoever You Be of the sonnet—or someone who saw himself so portrayed, because in God's Madrid the cuckolded walked in double lines—escorted by a friend, came up to seek an explanation on the steps of San Felipe. The matter was resolved at nightfall with a taste of steel behind the wall of Los Recoletos, so thoroughly that both the presumed betrayed husband, as well as the friend—once their respective chest wounds had healed—turned to prose and never looked at a sonnet for the rest of their lives.

That morning on the steps of San Felipe, the general topic of conversation was the Prince of Wales and the infanta, alternating with the latest rumors from court on the war, which was reviving in Flanders. I recall that it was a sunny day, and that the sky was very blue and clean above the roof tiles of the nearby houses, and that the *mentidero* was a beehive of activity. Captain Alatriste continued to show himself in public without apparent fear—and now the hand that had been bandaged after the affair at the Gate of Lost Souls had healed. That day he was unobtrusive in dark hose, gray breeches, and a doublet fastened to the neck, and although the morning was warm, he was also wearing a cape to cover the grip of the pistol stuck in the back of his belt, in addition to his usual dagger and sword. Unlike most of the veteran soldiers of the period, Diego Alatriste was not fond of colorful adornments or trim, and the only bright note in his ensemble was the red plume in the band of his wide-brimmed hat. Even so, his appearance contrasted with the sobriety of don Francisco de Quevedo's dark clothing, brightened only by the cross of Santiago showing beneath the short cape, also black, that we called a *herreruelo*.

I had been allowed to accompany them, and had just run some errands at the Estafeta. The rest of the group had already gathered: Licenciado Calzas, Juan Vicuña, Dómine Pérez, and a few acquaintances who chatted at the railing of the steps overlooking Calle Mayor. The bone they were chewing was the latest impertinence of Buckingham, who—they had on good authority—had the brass to be disporting himself with the wife of the Conde de Olivares.

"Perfidious Albion!" declaimed Licenciado Calzas, who had not been able to abide the English for years. Once, returning from the Indies, he had come close to being captured by Walter Raleigh, a corsair who had splintered a mast and killed fifteen men.

"Harsh treatment," opined Vicuña, making a fist with his one remaining hand. "The only thing those heretics understand is harsh treatment. So *that* is how he repays the hospitality of our lord and king!"

Those grouped around him nodded circumspectly, among them two purported veterans with fierce mustaches who had never heard a harquebus fired in their lives; two or three idlers; a tall student from Salamanca named Juan Manuel de Parada, or de Pradas, who was wrapped in a threadbare cape and whose face spoke of hunger; a young painter recently arrived in Madrid and recommended to don Francisco by his friend Juan de Fonseca; and a cobbler from Calle Montera named Tabarca, famous for leading the *mosqueteros*—the rowdy hoi polloi at the theater who stood in the open space at the back of the yard to watch the play, applauding or whistling their disapproval and thereby determining its success or failure. Although of lowly birth, and illiterate, this Tabarca was a man to be reckoned with. He presented himself as a supreme authority, an old Christian and hidalgo down on his luck—as nearly everyone was—and because of his influence among the rabble in the open-air theaters, he was flattered by authors attempting to make their name at court, and even by some who already had.

"At any rate," Calzas put in with a cynical wink, "I have heard that the wife of the favorite is not a bad judge of blades. And Buckingham is a fine specimen of a man."

Dómine Pérez was scandalized. "Please God, Señor Licenciado! Curb your tongue. I know the lady's confessor, and I can assure you that Señora doña Inés de Zúñiga is a pious woman. A saint."

"And saints," Calzas impudently replied, "always get a rise out of our king."

He laughed maliciously, watching the *dómine* cross himself as he looked nervously around. For his part, Captain Alatriste was frowning at Calzas disapprovingly for speaking so frankly in my presence. The likable young painter named Diego de Silva, a Sevillano with a heavy accent, was observing us as if wondering what he had gotten himself into.

"With your leave, Your Mercies," he began timidly, lifting an index finger stained with oil paint.

But no one paid much attention to him. Despite his friend Fonseca's recommendation, don Francisco de Quevedo had not forgotten that the minute the young artist reached Madrid, he had painted a portrait of Luis de Góngora, and although he had no reason not to like the youth, he meant to purge that capital sin by ignoring him for a few days. Although the truth is that don Francisco and the young Sevillian were soon as thick as thieves, and the best portrait we have of the poet is precisely the one that the same young man later painted. Over time, he also became a very good friend to Diego Alatriste and to me, but that was when he was better known by his mother's family name: Velázquez.

Well, then. I was telling you that after the painter's unfruitful attempt to intervene in the conversation, someone brought up the question of the Palatinate, and everyone dived into an animated discussion of Spanish politics in central Europe, in which the cobbler Tabarca threw in his jack of spades with all the assurance in the world, giving his opinion on Maximilian of Bavaria, the Prince Elector of the Palatinate, and the Pope of Rome, who, it was generally agreed, had a secret agreement. One purported *miles gloriosus* (and here a bow to Plautus) swore that he had the latest word on the matter, passed on to him by a brother-in-law of his who served in the palace . . . but that conversation was interrupted when all the men, except the *dómine*, leaned over the railing to greet some ladies passing in an open carriage. Buried in a pouf of skirts, brocades, and farthingales, they were on their way to the silver shops at the Guadalajara gate: they were harlots, but very high-class harlots. In our Spain of the Austrias, even whores put on airs.

The men donned their hats again and continued their conversation. Quevedo, who was not listening very carefully, moved a little closer to Alatriste and pointed his bearded chin toward two individuals standing some distance away.

"Are they following you, Captain?" he asked in a low voice, looking off in the opposite direction. "Or are they following me?"

Alatriste chanced a discreet glance toward the pair. They had the look of bailiffs, or hired "problem solvers." When they realized they were being watched, they turned slightly away.

"I would say that they are following me, don Francisco. But considering your verses, one never knows."

The poet looked at my master, frowning. "Let us suppose that it is you. Is it serious?"

"It may be."

"By my oath, it must be so. In that case there is no choice but to fight! Do you need my assistance?"

"No, not at the moment." The captain studied the swordsmen through half-closed eyes, as if attempting to engrave their faces in his memory. "Besides, you have enough trouble without taking on mine."

For a few seconds don Francisco said nothing. Then he twirled his mustache and, after adjusting his eyeglasses, stared openly, angrily, at the two strangers. "In any case," he concluded, "if there *is* a challenge, two and two would make an even fight. You may count on me."

"I know," said Alatriste.

"*Ziss, zass!* We will take care of them." The poet rested his hand on the pommel of his sword, which was poking up the hem of his cape. "I owe you that much, and more. And my maestro is not exactly Pacheco."

The captain shared his malicious smile. Luis Pacheco de Narváez was reputed to be the best fencing master in Madrid, having become the instructor of our lord and king. He had written several treatises on weapons, and once when he was in the home of the president of Castile, he had argued with don Francisco de Quevedo about several points and conclusions. As a result, they took up swords for a friendly demonstration, and don Francisco made the first move, striking Maestro Pacheco on the head and dislodging his hat. From that moment on, the enmity between the two men was legend: one had denounced the other before the tribunal of the Inquisition, and that one had portrayed *him*, with little charity, in *The Life of a Petty Thief Named Pablos*, which although it was printed two or three years later, was already circulating in manuscript copies throughout Madrid.

"Here comes Lope!" someone said.

To a man, they doffed their hats when the great Félix Lope de Vega Carpio was seen strolling toward them amid the greetings of people standing back to let him pass. He paused a few moments to converse with don Francisco de Quevedo, who congratulated him on the play to be performed the next day in El Príncipe. Diego Alatriste had promised to take me to this important theater event, the first play I would see in my life. Then don Francisco made some introductions.

"Captain don Diego Alatriste y Tenorio . . . You already know Juan Vicuña. . . . This is Diego de Silva. . . . The lad is Íñigo Balboa, son of a soldier killed in Flanders."

When he heard that, Lope patted my head with a spontaneous gesture of sympathy. It was the first time I had seen him, although I would later have other opportunities. I will always remember him as a grave sixty-year-old with distinguished bearing, a dignified figure clad in clerical black, with a lean face, short, nearly white hair, gray mustache, and a cordial, somewhat distracted, almost weary smile that he bestowed on one and all before continuing on his way, surrounded by murmurs of respect.

"Do not ever forget that man or this day," the captain said, giving me an affectionate rap on the spot where Lope had touched me.

And I never forgot. Still today, so many years later, I put my hand to the crown of my head and feel the affectionate touch of the Phoenix of Geniuses. All of them—he, don Francisco de Quevedo, Velázquez, Captain Alatriste, the miserable and magnificent epoch I knew—all are gone now. But in libraries, in books, on canvases, in churches, in palaces, streets, and plazas, those men left an indelible mark that lives on. The memory of Lope's hand will disappear with me when I die, as will Velázquez's Andalusian accent, the sound of don Francisco's golden spurs jingling as he limped along, the serene gray-green gaze of Captain Alatriste. Yet the echoes of their singular lives will resound as long as that many-faceted country, that mix of towns, tongues, histories, bloods, and betrayed dreams exists: that marvelous and tragic stage we call Spain.

Neither have I forgotten what happened a little later. The hour of the Angelus was approaching and San Felipe was still buzzing when, just in front of the small shops below, I saw a carriage pull to a stop—a carriage I knew very well. I had been leaning on the railing of the steps, a little separated from my elders but close enough to hear what they were saying.

The eyes looking up—at me—seemed to reflect the color of the magnificent sky far above our heads. They were so blue that everything around me except that color, that sky, that gaze, evaporated from my consciousness. It was like a delectable torment of blueness and light, a lagoon that was impossible to pull myself from. If I am to die someday—I thought at that instant—this is how I want to die: drowning in that color. I eased a little farther away from the group and slowly went down the stairs, almost as if I had no will of my own, or had swallowed a philter brewed by Hypnos.

And as I walked down the San Felipe steps to Calle Mayor, I could feel upon me—for an instant, like a flash of lucidity in the midst of my rapture, from thousands of leagues away—the worried eyes of Captain Alatriste.

X. EL PRÍNCIPE CORRAL

I fell right into the trap. Or to be more exact, five minutes of conversation was all it took for them to bait it. Even now, after so many years, I want to believe that Angélica de Alquézar was just a girl manipulated by her elders, but not even knowing her as I later knew her can I be sure. Always, to the day of her death, I sensed in her something that no one can learn from another person: an evil, cold wisdom that you see in some women from the time they are girls. Even before that; perhaps for centuries. Deciding who was truly responsible for all that followed is another matter, one that would take a while to analyze, and this is not the place or time. We can sum it up by saying, for now, that of the weapons that God and nature gave woman to defend herself from the stupidity and baseness of man, Angélica de Alquézar had far more than her share.

The afternoon of the next day, on the way back from El Príncipe theater, I was remembering her as I had seen her the previous day at the window of the black carriage stopped beneath the steps of San Felipe. Something had struck a false note, as when, in a musical performance that seems perfect, you detect an uncertain chord. All I had done was go over and exchange a few words, enchanted by her mysterious smile and golden curls. Without getting out of the carriage, while her chaperone was occupied in purchasing a few items in the little shops and the coachman seemed absorbed with his mules—that alone should have put me on guard—Angélica de Alquézar again had thanked me for my help in scattering the ragamuffins on Calle Toledo, asked me how I was getting along with my Captain Batiste, or Triste, and inquired about my life and my plans. I strutted a little, I confess. Those wide blue eyes that seemed to take an interest in everything I was saying prodded me to say more than I should have. I spoke of Lope, whom I had just met on the steps, as if he were an old friend. And I mentioned my intention to attend *El Arenal of Seville*, the play being performed the next day at El Príncipe. We chatted a bit, I asked her name, and after hesitating a delicious instant, tapping her lips with a small fan, she told me.

"Angélica comes from 'angel,'" I commented, enslaved. She looked at me with amusement and said nothing for a long while. I felt as if I had been transported to the gates of Paradise. Then her chaperone returned, the coachman caught sight of me, slapped the reins, drove off, and I was left standing there, frozen among the passing parade, feeling as though I had been brutally ripped from some magical place.

Only later that night, when I could not sleep for thinking of her, and the next day on the way back from the theater, did some peculiar details occur to me. No well-brought-up girl was permitted to chat, right in plain sight, with young nobodies she scarcely knew. I began to sense that I was teetering on the brink of something dangerous and unknown. I even asked myself whether Angélica's attention to me could have been connected with the eventful hours of some nights earlier. However you looked at it, any relation between that blonde angel and the ruffians at the Gate of Lost Souls seemed unimaginable. Added to that, the prospect of attending a play by Lope had clouded my judgment. And that, says the Turk, is how God blinds those He wants to go astray.

From the monarch to the lowest townsman, in the Spain of Philip the Fourth, everyone had a burning passion for theater. The *comedias* had three *jornadas*, or acts, and were written in verse, in several meters and rhymes. Their hallowed authors, as we have seen in the case of Lope, were loved and respected, and the popularity of the actors and actresses was enormous. Every premiere or performance of a famous work brought out town and court, and through the nearly three hours each play lasted, the audience was in thrall. At that time, the productions usually took place in daylight, in the afternoon after the midday meal, in open-air venues know as *corrales*. There were two in Madrid: El Príncipe, also known as La Pacheca, and La Cruz. Lope preferred the stage of the latter, which was also the favorite of our lord and king, who loved the theater as much as his wife, Elizabeth of France, did. And just as much as our monarch loved theater, being especially fond of youthful adventures, he also loved, clandestinely, the beautiful actresses of the moment—chief among them María Calderón, or La Calderona, who gave him a son, the second don Juan of Austria.

Expectation was high that day. One of Lope's celebrated *comedias* was playing at El Príncipe! Long before it started, animated groups of theatergoers were wending their way toward the *corral,* and by noon the narrow street on which it was then located—across from the convent of Santa Ana—was already crowded. The captain and I had met Juan Vicuña and Licenciado Calzas along the way; they, too, were great admirers of Lope's, and don Francisco de Quevedo had joined us on the same street. So we all went on together to the gate of the theater, where it became nearly impossible to move among the crowd. Every level of society was represented: The elite occupied the boxes over-looking the stage and the benches and standing room for the public, while those further down the social ladder filled the tiers below the boxes and the wooden benches in the yard. Women sat in their own gallery, the *cazuela*; the sexes were separated in the *corral* as in church. And behind a dividing barrier, the open yard was reserved for those who stood throughout the play: the famous *mosqueteros*, there with their spiritual leader, the cobbler Tabarca. When he passed our group he greeted us gravely, solemnly, puffed up with his own importance.

By two o'clock, Calle El Príncipe and the entrances to the *corral* were swarming with merchants, artisans, pages, students, clergy, scribes, soldiers, lackeys, squires, and ruffians who had dressed for the occasion in cape, sword, and dagger, all calling themselves caballeros and ready to clash over a place to watch the play. Added to that seething, fascinating commotion were the women, who swept into the *cazuela* amid a flurry of skirts, shawls, and fans, and were pinned like butterflies by the eyes of every gallant twirling his mustaches in the boxes and yard. The women, too, quarreled over their seats, and at times an official had to intervene and establish peace in the spaces reserved for them. Confrontations over someone's having slipped in without paying, and squabbles between the person who had reserved a seat and another person who claimed it frequently provoked a "How dare you?" backed with a sword, all of which demanded the presence of a magistrate and attending bailiffs.

Not even nobles were above these altercations. The Duque de Fera and Duque de Rioseco, disputing the favors of an actress, had once knifed each other in the middle of a play; they claimed that it was over their seats. Licenciado Luis Quiñones, a timid and good man from Toledo who was a friend of Captain Alatriste's and mine, described, in one of his irreverent ballads, the ambience that lent itself to slashing and stabbing:

> *They come to the* corral de comedias
> *Pouring in like rain, and soaking wet.*
> *But if they slip in without paying,*
> *They leave streaming blood—and wetter yet!*

Strange people, we. As someone would later write, confronting danger, dueling, defying authority, gambling life or liberty are things that have always been done, in every corner of the world, whether for hunger, hatred, lust, honor, or patriotism. But to put hand to sword, or to knife another being, merely to get into a theater performance was something reserved for the Spain of my youth. When good, it was very good, but when bad, far worse than bad. It was the era of quixotic, sterile deeds that determined reason and right at the imperious tip of a sword.

As we made our way to the *corral*, we had to thread through groups of early arrivals, and beggars harassing everyone who passed by. Of course, half of the blind, lame, amputee, and maimed were malingerers, self-proclaimed hidalgos brought down to begging because of an unfortunate accident. You had to excuse yourself with a courteous "I'm sorry, sir, I am not carrying any money" if you did not want to be berated in a most unpleasant fashion. The manner of begging is different among different peoples. The Germans beg in a group, the French are servile, reciting orisons and pleas, the Portuguese implore with lamentations, the Italians with long tales of misfortunes and ills, and the Spanish with arrogance and threats—saucy, insolent, and impatient.

We paid a quarter-*maravedí* at the entrance, three *maravedís* at the second door, for hospital charity, and twenty *maravedís* for a seat on the benches. Naturally our places were occupied, although we had paid a lot for them, but not wanting to get into a scuffle with me along, the captain, don Francisco, and the others decided that we would sit at the back, close to the *mosqueteros*. I was wide-eyed, taking everything in, fascinated by the people, the vendors of mead and sweetmeats, the buzz of conversations, the whirl of farthingales, skirts, and petticoats in the women's galleries, the elegance of the well-to-do visible at the windows of their boxes. It was said that the king himself often sat there, incognito, when the play was to his taste. And the presence that afternoon of members of the royal guard on the stairs, not wearing uniforms but looking as if they were on duty, seemed to hint at that possibility.

We kept our eyes on the boxes, hoping to discover our young monarch there, or the queen, but we did not recognize any of the aristocratic faces that occasionally peered from between the lattices. The person we did see, however, was Lope himself, whom the public loudly applauded. We also glimpsed the Conde de Guadalmedina, accompanied by some friends and ladies, and Álvaro de la Marca, who responded with a courteous smile as Captain Alatriste touched the brim of his hat in greeting.

Some friends offered don Francisco de Quevedo a place on a bench, and he excused himself and went to join them. Juan Vicuña and Licenciado Calzas were some distance away, discussing the work we were going to see, which Calzas had enjoyed years before at its first performance. As for Diego Alatriste, he was with me, having made a place for me on the barrier separating us from the open yard, so I could see without obstacle. He had bought fried bread with cinnamon and honey that I was crunching with delight, and had a hand on my shoulder to prevent me from being jostled off my place on the barrier. Suddenly I felt his grip tighten, and he slowly withdrew his hand and rested it on the pommel of his sword.

I followed the direction of his eyes, which had turned steely gray, and among the crowd made out the two men who had been lounging about on the steps of San Felipe the day before. They were standing in the pack of *mosqueteros* and I thought I saw them exchange some kind of sign with two other men who had taken up positions not too far away. The hats tilted to one side, the folded capes, the long curled mustaches and beards, a scar or two, and their way of cutting their eyes from side to side and standing with their legs planted firmly apart were sure signs of men acquainted with a knife. The *corral* was filled with such men, it is true, but those four seemed singularly interested in us.

I heard the thumps that signaled the start of the *comedia*, the *mosqueteros* shouted *"Sombreros!"* and then all doffed their hats. The curtain was drawn, and my attention flew like metal to magnet from the ruffians to the stage, where the characters of doña Laura and Urbana, both wearing cloaks, were entering. In front of the backdrop, a small pasteboard construction represented the Torre del Oro.

"Famous is El Arenal."
"I must say I find you right."
"In my view, there cannot be
In all the world a finer sight."

I still get a thrill when I remember those lines, the first
I ever heard on the stage of a *corral,* and I remember even
more clearly because the actress who played doña Laura
was the very beautiful María de Castro, who was later to
fill a certain space in the lives of Captain Alatriste and me.
But that day in El Príncipe, she was the beautiful Laura,
who accompanies her uncle Urbana to the port of Seville,
where the galleys are about to set sail, and where, by
chance, she meets don Lope, and Toledo, his servant.

"I must make haste, my ship sails
Just following the ebb.
Ah, what victory it is to flee
A scheming woman's web!"

Everything around me vanished; I was completely absorbed in the words coming from the mouths of the actors.
Within minutes I was transported to El Arenal, madly in
love with Laura, and wishing I had the gallantry of
Captains Fajardo and Castellanos, and that I were the one

crossing swords with the bailiffs and catchpoles before sailing off in the king's Armada, saying, as don Lope does,

> *"I had to call upon my sword.*
> *To honor an hidalgo who*
> *Insults me, I must draw my sword;*
> *A point of honor, it is true,*
> *A code we have both lived since birth.*
> *To refuse to duel a man who vents*
> *His anger against you, even*
> *A lunatic, if he gives offense,*
> *Is not to give a man his worth."*

It was at that moment that one of the spectators standing beside us turned toward the captain and hissed at him to be quiet, although he had not said a word. I turned, surprised, and saw that the captain was staring intently at the man who had hushed him, a rough-looking individual whose cape was folded four times over one shoulder and whose hand was on the grip of his sword.

The play continued, and I was again drawn into it. Although Diego Alatriste was neither talking nor moving, the man with the folded cape again hissed at him, muttering in a low voice about people who had no respect for the theater or for letting other people hear. I felt the captain's hand, which was again resting on my shoulder, softly push me to one side, and I noticed that he pulled back his cape a little, to uncover the handle of the dagger in a sheath at his left side. At that instant, the first act ended, the public burst into applause, and the captain and our neighbor bored holes into each other with their eyes, though for the moment things went no further. There was one ruffian on either side, and, a short distance away, the other four, who kept us firmly in their view.

During the dance performed in the entr'acte, the captain caught the eye of Vicuña and Calzas and put me in their care, using the pretext that I could see the second *jornada* better from where they were watching. There was a sudden burst of deafening applause, and we all turned toward one of the upper boxes, where people had recognized our lord and king, who had quietly entered at the beginning of the previous act. For the first time, I saw his pale features, the blond wavy hair that fell over his brow and temples, and the mouth with the prominent lower lip so characteristic of the Hapsburgs, still bare of the straight beard he would later adopt. Our monarch was dressed in black velvet, with a starched ruff and discreet silver buttons—faithful to the decree of austerity at court that he himself had just issued—and in his slender hand, so pale the blue veins showed through the skin, he casually held a chamois glove, which he occasionally put to his mouth to hide a smile or words directed to his companions.

Among these the enthusiastic public had recognized, besides several Spanish gentlemen, the Prince of Wales and Buckingham, whom His Majesty—though maintaining official incognito—had thought it well to invite; all wore their hats, as if the king were not present. The grave sobriety of the Spaniards contrasted with the plumes, ribbons, bows, and jewels of the two Englishmen, whose bearing and youth were greatly celebrated by the public, and the source of no few compliments, fluttering of fans, and devastating glances from the women's *cazuela*.

The second act began. As during the first, I sat drinking in the actors' every word and gesture. Yet just as Captain Fajardo was saying,

> "'Cousin' he calls her. I do not know
> If this cousin is a true one;
> But she is not the first young girl
> To be falsely claimed a cousin,"

the swaggerer with the cape over his shoulder once again hissed at Diego Alatriste, and this time he was joined by two of the other four troublemakers, who had inched closer during the entr'acte. The captain himself had played the same game more than once, so to him what they were doing was as clear as water, especially considering that the two remaining swashbucklers were now elbowing through the *mosqueteros*.

The captain looked around to assess the situation. It was significant that neither the magistrate nor the bailiffs who usually imposed order during performances were any-where to be seen. As for other help, Licenciado Calzas was not a man-of-arms, and the fifty-year-old Juan Vicuña could not do much with just one hand. Don Francisco de Quevedo was two rows ahead of us, focused on the stage and unaware of what was brewing behind him. And the worst of it was that some of the public, influenced by the hissing of the provocateurs, began to scowl at Alatriste as if he truly were disturbing the performance. What was about to happen was as obvious as two and two make four. Or in that specific case, three and two make five. And five to one was too much, even for the captain.

Alatriste tried to ease toward the nearest door. If forced to fight, he could do so more freely outside than inside the theater, where in the time it takes to breathe *"Jesús!"* he was going to be stitched like a quilt by daggers. There were two churches nearby, where he could find sanctuary if the law intervened in time. But since the unholy five were al-ready closing in, the business was taking an ugly turn.

That was the situation as the second act ended.

Applause resounded, and the insults of the miscreants grew louder. Now the rabble began to chime in. Words were exchanged, and the tone heated up.

Finally, between oaths and "By my lifes," someone uttered the word "blackguard." Then Diego Alatriste sighed deeply, down to his toes. That sealed it. With resignation, he gripped his sword and withdrew steel from scabbard.

At least, he thought fleetingly as he bared his blade, a couple of those whoresons would accompany him to Hell. Without even setting himself firmly, he cut a swath to the right to drive back the nearest ruffian, and reaching back with his left hand, he pulled the *vizcaína* from where it was sheathed over his kidneys. People around him scrambled to get out of the way, women in the *cazuela* screamed, and the occupants of the boxes leaned over the railing to see better. It was not unusual at that time, as I have said, for the entertainment to shift from the stage to the yard, so everyone settled in to enjoy a bonus performance; within moments, a circle had formed around the contenders.

The captain, sure that he could not long defend himself against five armed and skillful men, decided not to concern himself with the fine points of fencing; the best way to maintain his health was to impair that of his enemies. He took one stab at the man with the folded cape, and without stopping to see the result—which was not significant—he stooped low, hoping with his *vizcaína* to cut the hamstring of another opponent. If you do the arithmetic, five swords and five daggers add up to ten weapons slicing through the air, so the stabs and thrusts were raining down like hail. One came so close that it cut a sleeve of the captain's doublet, and another would have gone through his body had it not become tangled in his cape. Attacking right and left with coups and *moulinets,* Alatriste forced two of his adversaries to retreat, parried one with his sword and another with his knife, then felt the cold, sharp edge of a blade being drawn across his head. Blood streamed down between his eyebrows.

You are fucked, Diego, he told himself with a last shred of lucidity. This is it. And it was true, he felt exhausted. His arms were as heavy as lead, and he was blinded by blood. He raised his left hand, the one with the dagger, to swipe the blood from his eyes, and saw a sword pointed toward his throat. And in that same instant he heard don Francisco de Quevedo yelling, "Alatriste! He's mine! He's mine!" in a voice like thunder. He had leaped from the benches to the barrier, and interposed his sword, blocking the deadly thrust.

"Five to two is a little better!" the poet exclaimed, sword raised, with a happy nod to the captain. "We have no choice but to fight!"

And in fact, he fought like the demon he was, Toledo sword tight in his grip, and completely unimpeded by his lameness. Undoubtedly verses and figures for the *décima* he would compose if he came out of this alive were racing through his mind. His eyeglasses had fallen to his chest and were dangling from their ribbon near the red cross of Santiago; he was sweating hard, ferociously venting the bile that he usually reserved for his verses but that on occasions like this he expressed with the point of his sword. His dramatic and unexpected charge subdued the attackers, and he even succeeded in wounding one of them with a good thrust that went through the band of the man's baldric and into the shoulder. Recovering from their shock, the attackers regained their focus and closed in again, and the battle continued in a whirlwind of steel. Even the actors came out on the stage to watch.

What happened next is history. Witnesses report that, in the box where the supposedly incognito king, Wales, Buckingham, and their train of courtiers were sitting, everyone was watching the altercation below with great interest, though with conflicting emotions. Our monarch, as was natural, was annoyed by the shameful affront to public order in his august presence, even though that presence was not official. But the young, daring, and chivalrous part of his being was not, in a deeper sense, greatly disturbed that his foreign guests were witnessing a spontaneous demonstration of courage on the part of his subjects, men whom, after all, they usually met on the field of battle.

One thing could not be disputed, and that was that the man fighting against five was doing so with unbelievable desperation and courage, and that after only a few slashes and thrusts he had drawn the sympathy of the audience and shouts of anguish among the ladies when they saw him so sorely pressed.

Our lord and king was torn, it was later reported, between protocol and enjoyment, and therefore was slow to order the head of his civilian-clad escort to intervene and put an end to the disturbance. And just as finally he opened his mouth to give a royal, uncontestable order, to everyone's surprise and admiration, don Francisco de Quevedo, who was very well known at court, jumped resolutely into the fray.

But the greatest surprise was still to come. The poet had shouted the name Alatriste as he entered the tournament, and our lord and king, aghast at every new development, noticed that when Buckingham and Charles of England heard that name, they turned to look at each other with a start of recognition.

"Ala-tru-iste!" exclaimed the Prince of Wales, with his childish British pronunciation. And after leaning over the railing an instant, he quickly assessed the situation in the yard below, again turned to Buckingham, and then the king. In the days he had spent in Madrid he had had time to learn a few words and phrases of Spanish, and using them, he apologized and excused himself to the king.

"*Diess-culpad, Si-yure*. . . . I am indebted to that man. He saved my life."

Even as he spoke, as phlegmatic and serene as if he were at Saint James's Palace, he removed his hat, adjusted his gloves, and asking for his sword looked at Buckingham with perfect sangfroid.

"Steenie," he said.

Then, without hesitation, steel in hand, he raced down the stairs, followed by Buckingham, who was pulling out his sword. An astonished Philip did not know whether to stop them or go to the railing to watch, so that by the time he recovered the composure he had been so close to losing, the two Englishmen were already in the yard of the *corral de comedias*, crossing swords with the five men who had Francisco de Quevedo and Diego Alatriste boxed in.

It was a combat of which epics are made. Boxes, galleries, *cazuela*, benches, and yard—all stupefied to see Charles and Buckingham appear with weapons in hand—exploded with a roar of applause and shouts of approval. With that, our lord and king reacted, rose to his feet, turned to his courtiers, and ordered them to end the madness. As he gave the order, his glove dropped to the floor. And that, in someone who ruled forty-four years without ever raising an eyebrow or changing expression in public, betrayed how that afternoon in El Príncipe *corral,* the monarch of both the new world and the old came within an ace of revealing emotion.

XI. THE SEAL AND THE LETTER

Through a window that opened onto one of the large court-
yards of the Alcázar Real, the crisp shouts of the Spanish,
Burgundian, and German troops reached Diego Alatriste's
ears as the guard was changed at the palace gates. There
was a single carpet on the wood floor of the room, and on
it an enormous dark table covered with papers, files, and
books, as somber as the man seated behind it. This man was
methodically reading letters and dispatches, one after another, and from time to time he wrote something in a mar-
gin with a quill he dipped into a Talavera pottery inkwell.
He worked without stopping, as if ideas were flowing
across the paper as smoothly as his reading, or the ink. This
went on for a long while.

The man did not look up even when the head constable, Martín Saldaña, accompanied by the sergeant and two

soldiers of the royal guard who had brought Diego Alatriste through secret corridors, led him in and then withdrew. The man at the table continued dispatching letters, unperturbed, as if he were alone, so the captain had all the time in the world to study him. He was corpulent, with a large head and a ruddy face; coarse black hair fell over his ears, and his chin and cheeks were covered by a thick dark beard and enormous mustache. He was clad in dark blue silk trimmed with black braid, and his shoes and hose were black as well. On his chest blazed the red cross of Calatrava, which along with the white ruff and a handsome gold chain was the only contrast to his somber attire.

Although Gaspar de Guzmán, third Conde de Olivares, would not be made a duke until two years later, he was enjoying his second year of favor at court. At age thirty-five, he was a grandee of Spain, and his power was enormous. The young monarch, much fonder of fiestas and hunting than of affairs of government, was a blind instrument in Guzmán's hands, and any who might have overshadowed him were either crushed or dead. His former protectors, the Duque de Uceda and Fray Luis de Aliaga, favorites of the previous king, found themselves in exile; the Duque de Osuna was in disgrace, with his properties confiscated; the Duque de Lerma had escaped the gibbet thanks to his cardinal's robes—*He whose cape is cardinal red will not hang by the neck until he's dead*, was the old saying—and

Rodrigo Calderón, another of the principals in the former regime, had been executed in the public plaza. Now no one stood in the way of that intelligent, cultured, patriotic, and ambitious man's design to hold in his hands the strings of the empire that was still the most powerful on earth.

It is easy enough to imagine the emotions Diego Alatriste was experiencing as he stood before this all-powerful favorite of the king in that huge chamber in which, except for the table and carpet, the only decoration, mounted above a large unlighted fireplace, was a portrait of Philip the Second, grandfather of the present monarch. The captain's apprehension grew after he recognized in the man at the table—without the least doubt or pause to consider—the taller and stronger of the two masked men from that first night at the Santa Bárbara gate. The same man whom the one with the round head had called Excellency before his superior left, after requesting that not too much blood be shed in the affair of the two Englishmen.

If only, the captain thought, the execution that lay in store for him would not be by garrote. It was not that dangling at the end of a rope was his cup of tea, either, but at least it was better than being removed with an ignominious tourniquet squeezing tighter and tighter around his neck, his face contorted as he heard the executioner say, "Forgive me, Your Mercy, I am only following orders."

May Christ unleash a thunderbolt to incinerate all the spineless lackeys who were "just following orders," and take with them the bastards who gave the orders as well. Not to mention the obligatory handcuffs, brazier, judge, reporter, scribe, and executioner needed to obtain a proper confession before speeding your disjointed body toward Hell. Diego Alatriste did not sing well with a rope around his neck, so his last serenade would be long and painful. Given a choice, he would have preferred to end his days with steel, fighting. That was, after all, the decent way for a soldier to make his exit: *Viva España!* and all that, and little angels singing his way in Heaven, or wherever he was to go.

"But not many blessings are being handed out these days," a worried Martín Saldaña had whispered to him when he came to wake him at the prison that early morning and take him to the Alcázar.

"By my faith, it looks bad this time, Diego."

"I have had it worse."

"No. Not ever. The person who wants to see you allows no man to save himself by his sword."

Worse, Alatriste had nothing to fight *with*. Even the slaughterer's knife in his boot had been taken from him when he was imprisoned after the row in the *corral de comedias*, when the intervention of the Englishmen had at least prevented him from being killed on the spot.

"En pas ahora este-unos"—we're even now—Charles of England had said when the guard arrived to separate the contenders, or protect him, which in reality was one and the same. And after sheathing his sword, he, along with Buckingham, had turned away, acting as if he were completely unaware of the applause of an admiring public. Don Francisco de Quevedo was allowed to go, by the personal order of the king, who apparently had been pleased with his latest sonnet. As for the five swordsmen, two escaped in the confusion, one had been carried off gravely wounded, and the other two were arrested at the same time as Alatriste and put in the cell next to his. As the captain left that morning with Saldaña, he had passed by that same cell. Empty.

The Conde de Olivares continued to focus on his correspondence, and the captain looked toward the window, with somber hope. That out might save him from the executioner and shorten the process, although a thirty-foot fall from the window to the courtyard might not be enough; he might merely expose himself to the torment of ending up injured but alive, and hoisted onto the mule to hang, broken legs and all, which was not a pretty picture. And there was yet another problem: What if there was Someone up there after all? He would hold Alatriste's jumping to his death against him all through an afterlife no less unpleasant for being hypothetical.

So if the bugles were blowing *Retreat!* it was better to go having had the sacraments, and dispatched by another hand. Just in case. When all was said and done, he consoled himself, however painful, and however long it takes to die, in the end you are just as dead. And he who dies finds rest.

He was mulling over these happy thoughts when he became aware that the court favorite had finished his task and had turned his attention to him. Those fiery black eyes seemed to be taking in every detail. Alatriste, whose doublet and hose showed the signs of the night spent in a cell, regretted that he did not present a better appearance. A clean bandage over the slash on his forehead would have helped, and water to wash away the dried blood on his face.

"Have you seen me before, do you think?"

Olivares's question caught the captain unawares. A sixth sense, something like the sound a steel blade makes when drawn over a whetstone, warned him to display exquisite caution.

"No. Never."

"Never?"

"I have said so, Excellency."

"Not even during some public function?"

"Well . . ." the captain stroked his mustache, as if trying hard to remember. "Perhaps . . . in the Plaza Mayor, or at the Hieronymite convent . . . someplace like that." He nodded with what passed as thoughtful honesty. "That is possible, yes."

Olivares held his eyes, impassive. "No other time?"

"No, no other time."

For a very brief instant the captain believed he glimpsed a smirk in the favorite's thick growth of beard. But he was never sure. Olivares had picked up one of the files on his table and was leafing through the pages distractedly.

"You served in Flanders and Naples, I see here. And against the Turks in the Levant, and on the Barbary coast. A long life as a soldier."

"Since I was thirteen, Excellency."

"Your title of captain is, I imagine, unearned?"

"Not officially. I never rose above the rank of sergeant, and I was relieved of that after a . . . scuffle."

"Yes, that is what it says here." The minister kept riffling through the documents. "You quarreled with a lieutenant—in fact, you ran him through. I am surprised that you were not hanged for that."

"They were going to, Excellency. But that same day in Maastricht our troops mutinied. They had not been paid for five months. I myself did not join them, fortunately, so I had the opportunity to defend Field Marshal Miguel de Orduña from his own soldiers."

"You do not approve of mutinies?"

"I do not like to see officers murdered."

His questioner arched an eyebrow peevishly. "Not even those who intend to hang you?"

"One thing is one thing, and another, another."

"To defend your field marshal, it says here, you put away another two or three with your sword."

"They were Tudescos, Excellency. Germans. And the field marshal told me, 'Devil take it, Alatriste. If I am going to be killed by mutineers, at least let them be Spanish.' I agreed with him, lent a hand, and that won my pardon."

Olivares was listening attentively. From time to time he looked at the papers and then at Diego Alatriste thoughtfully.

"I see," he said. "There is also a letter of recommendation from the former Conde de Guadalmedina, and a draft from don Ambrosio de Spínola signed in his hand, granting eight *escudos* extra pay for your good service in battle. Did you collect that?"

"No, Excellency. Generals give an order, and secretaries, administrators, and scribes execute it in their own manner. When I went to claim my *escudos*, they had been reduced to four, and even those I have not seen to this day."

The minister dipped his head slightly, as though he,

too, had had bonuses or salaries withheld. Or perhaps he was approving the reluctance of the secretaries, administrators, and scribes to release public monies. He kept leafing through papers with the meticulousness of a clerk.

"Discharged after Fleurus because of a serious, and honorable, wound," Olivares continued. Now he focused on the bandage on the captain's head. "You have a certain propensity for getting wounded, I see."

"And for wounding, Excellency."

Diego Alatriste stood a little straighter, twisting his mustache. It was obvious that he did not like for anyone—not even the person who could have him immediately executed—to take his wounds lightly. Olivares noted the insolent spark in the captain's eyes, and then turned back to the document.

"So it seems," he concluded. "Although the references to your adventures apart from service to the flag are less exemplary than your military record. I see here a fight in Naples that involved a death. Ah! And also insubordination during the repression of the Moorish rebels in Valencia." He frowned. "Perhaps you did not agree with the decree of expulsion signed by His Majesty?"

The captain hesitated before answering. "I was a soldier," he said after a bit. "Not a butcher."

"I imagined you to be a better servant of your king."

"And I am. I have served him even better than I have God, for I have broken God's commandments, but none of my king's."

Again the favorite crooked an eyebrow. "I always believed that the Valencia campaign was glorious."

"Then you were ill informed, Excellency. There is no glory whatsoever in sacking houses, violating women, and cutting the throats of defenseless civilians."

Olivares's expression was impenetrable. "All of them enemies of the true religion," he pointed out. "And unwilling to renounce Mohammed."

The captain shrugged. "Perhaps," he replied. "But that was not my fight."

"Come now"—the minister raised both eyebrows, with feigned surprise. "And to do murder for another party is?"

"I do not kill the young or the old, Excellency."

"I see. Which was why you left your company and enlisted in the galleys of Naples."

"Yes. Given the task of goring infidels, I preferred to do so against men who could defend themselves."

For a long moment, the once masked man sat without saying a word. Then he shifted his gaze to the papers on the table. He seemed to be turning Alatriste's last words over in his mind.

"Regardless of your record, however, it seems that there are men of quality who defend you," he said finally.

"Young Guadalmedina, for example. Or don Francisco de Quevedo, who, just yesterday, in his usual bizarre behavior, decided to set his verbs in the active voice—although you know that associating with Quevedo can be a help or a hindrance, according to the ups and downs of his fortunes." Olivares paused—a significant pause. "It also appears that young Buckingham believes he is in your debt." An even longer pause followed. "And the Prince of Wales as well."

"I know nothing of that." Again Alatriste shrugged, his expression unchanged. "But yesterday those gentlemen did more than repay a debt, real or imaginary."

Slowly, Olivares shook his head. "Apparently not." He seemed vexed. "This very morning, Charles of England was interested enough to inquire about you and your fate. Even our lord and king, who is still stunned over what took place, wishes to be informed of the outcome." He abruptly pushed the file to one side. "This creates a troublesome situation. Very delicate."

Now Olivares looked at Diego Alatriste as if wondering what to do with him. "A shame," he went on, "that those five bunglers did not carry out their assignment better. Whoever paid them was on the right track. In a certain way, that would have solved everything."

"I am sorry that I do not share your regrets, Excellency."

"I shall take note of that . . ." The minister's gaze had

changed; now it was even harder and more unreadable. "Is it true what they say, that a few days back you saved the life of a certain English traveler when a comrade of yours was about to kill him?"

Alarm. Sound the alarm with drumrolls and trumpets, thought Alatriste. This sudden shift was more dangerous than a night raid by the Dutch when an entire Spanish *tercio* was laid out snoring. Conversations like this could lead straight to having one's neck in a noose. At that moment he would not wager a pittance on his neck.

"Your Excellency must be mistaken. I do not remember such a happening."

"Well, it would be to your benefit to remember."

The captain had been threatened many times in his life, and in addition he was sure he would not emerge unscathed from this contest. So being lost in either case, he did not flinch. But that did not stand in the way of his choosing his words with great care.

"I do not know whether I saved anyone's life," he said after thinking a moment. "But I do recall that when I was hired for a certain service, my principal employer said that he did not want any deaths."

"Truly? That is what he said?"

"Yes, his very words."

Olivares's penetrating pupils were pointed at the captain like the bore of a harquebus. "And who was that *principal?*" he asked with dangerous softness.

Alatriste did not blink. "I have no idea, Excellency. He wore a mask."

Now Olivares observed the captain with renewed interest. "And if those were your orders, how is it that your companion dared go further?"

"I do not know what companion you are referring to, Excellency. But in any case, other gentlemen who accompanied that preeminent señor later gave different instructions."

"Others?" The minister seemed very interested in that plural. "'Sblood! I would like to have their names. Or their descriptions."

"I am afraid that is impossible. You will already have noticed, Excellency, that I have great problems with my memory. And the masks . . ."

He watched as Olivares struck the table, venting his impatience. The look that he gave Alatriste, though, was more evaluating than menacing. He seemed to be weighing something in his mind.

"I am beginning to have my fill of your bad memory. And I warn you that there are executioners capable of making the strongest man sing a tune."

"I beg of Your Excellency, look at me. Carefully."

Olivares, who had done nothing else, frowned, both irritated and surprised. From his expression, Alatriste believed that he was going to call the guard and have him
removed and hanged at that moment. But he did nothing.
He did not comment or speak, but only stared at the captain's face, as requested. Finally, something in the firm
chin or the cold, gray-green eyes, which had not blinked
once during the examination, seemed to persuade him.

"Perhaps you are right," he nodded. "I would be will-
ing to swear that you are the sort who forgets. Or does not
talk." He stared pensively at the papers on the table. "I
have matters to attend to," he said. "I hope you will not
mind waiting here a while more."

He got up then, and went to a bell-pull near a wall and
tugged it once. Then he sat down again, and paid no further attention to the captain.

Alatriste's sense that he knew the individual who answered the bell increased as soon as he heard his voice. By
my life . . . ! This, he mused, was beginning to resemble a
reunion of old friends. The only ones needed to complete
the crew were Fray Emilio Bocanegra and the Italian
swordsman. The man before him had a round head, on
which floated a few graying brown hairs. All his hair was
sparse: the sideburns halfway down his face, the thinly
trimmed beard from lower lip to chin, and the scraggly
mustache curling over cheeks streaked with red veins, like

the ones on his fat nose. He was wearing black, and the embroidered cross of Calatrava on his chest did nothing to improve the vulgarity of his appearance. His wilted ruff was far from clean, as were the ink-stained hands that resembled those of an amanuensis who had hit a run of good fortune; only the heavy gold ring on the little finger of his left hand spoke to his privileged state. The eyes, though, were sharp and intelligent, and the knowing, critical arch of the left eyebrow lent a crafty, dangerous tone to the expression—first surprised and then cold and scornful— that crossed his face when he saw Diego Alatriste.

It was none other than Luis de Alquézar, private secretary to king Philip the Fourth. And this time he was wearing no mask.

"To sum up," said Olivares. "We are dealing here with two conspiracies. One intended to give a lesson to certain English travelers and to relieve them of a bundle of secret documents. And another intended simply to assassinate them. Of the first I had some knowledge, I seem to remember. . . . But the second is practically new to me. Perhaps you, don Luis, as secretary to His Majesty and an expert observer in certain ministerial offices at court, may have heard something?"

The favorite of the king had spoken very slowly, taking

his time and leaving long pauses between his sentences, and never taking his eyes off the man he had summoned. The secretary stood before Olivares, wary, occasionally sneaking a glance at Diego Alatriste. The captain had stepped to one side, wondering where the devil all this was going to end. A gathering of shepherds, and one dead sheep? Or about to be.

Olivares had stopped talking and was waiting. Luis de Alquézar cleared his throat.

"I fear I will be of very little help to Your Eminence," he said, and in his meticulously cautious tone showed his discomfort at Alatriste's presence. "I, too, had heard something about the first conspiracy. As for the second . . ." He looked at the captain and his left eyebrow rose in a sinister arch, like an upraised Turkish scimitar. "I do not know what this, ahem, person, may have told you."

Olivares's fingers drummed impatiently on the table. "This, ahem, *person,* has said nothing. He is waiting here for me to deal with another matter."

Luis de Alquézar was slow to speak, processing what he had just heard. Once it was digested, he looked toward Alatriste, and then Olivares again.

"But . . ." he began.

"There are no buts."

Alquézar again cleared his throat. "As Your Eminence

has set forth such a delicate subject in the presence of a third party, I thought that . . ."

"You thought wrongly."

"Forgive me." The secretary looked at the papers on the table with an uneasy expression, as if expecting to find something alarming in them. He had paled noticeably. "But I do not know whether before a stranger I should . . ."

The favorite of the king lifted an authoritative hand. Alatriste, who was watching closely, would have sworn that Olivares was enjoying himself.

"You should."

Alquézar swallowed four times and again cleared his throat, this time noisily. "I am always at the service of Your Eminence." His skin went from an extreme pallor to a sudden flush, as though he were suffering attacks of cold and heat. "What I can imagine of that second conspiracy . . ."

"Try to imagine every detail, I beg you."

"Of course, Your Eminence." Alquézar's eyes were still futilely scrutinizing the minister's papers; his instinct as a functionary impelled him to seek in them the explanation of what was happening to him. "As I was saying, all I can imagine, or suppose, is that certain interests crossed paths along the way. The Church, for example?"

"The word 'church' is very broad. Were you referring to someone in particular?"

"Very well. There are some who have secular, as well as ecclesiastic, power. And they fervently disapprove of a heretic's—"

"I see," the minister interrupted. "You were referring to saintly men like Fray Emilio Bocanegra, for example."

Alatriste saw the king's secretary repress a sudden start.

"I have not named the holy father," said Alquézar, regaining his composure. "But now that Your Eminence has seen fit to mention him, I would say yes. By that I mean that, in fact, Fray Emilio may be one of those who does not look kindly upon an alliance with England."

"I am surprised that you did not come to consult me, if you were harboring such suspicions."

The secretary sighed, venturing a discreet conciliatory smile. The longer the conversation continued, and he tested which tack to take, the more artful and sure of himself he seemed to be.

"Your Eminence is aware of how it is at court. It is difficult to survive—walking the line between Tyrians and Trojans, you know. There are influences. Pressures. Besides, it is well known that Your Eminence is not among those who favor an alliance with England. It was, actually, all in your best interests."

"By His wounds, Alquézar! I swear to you that for such

'services' I have had more than one man hanged."
Olivares's glare bored through the royal secretary like a
lethal musket ball. "Although I imagine that the gold of
Richelieu, of Savoy and Venice, would not have persuaded
anyone otherwise."

The royal secretary's complicit and servile smile vanished as if by magic. "I cannot know to what Your
Eminence is referring."

"You do not know? How curious. My spies have confirmed the delivery of an important sum of money to some
person at court, but without identifying the recipient. All
this makes things a little clearer for me."

Alquézar placed a hand on the embroidered cross of
Calatrava. "I pray that Your Eminence does not believe
that I . . ."

"You?" Olivares gave a dismissive wave, as if to brush
away a fly, causing Alquézar to smile with relief. "I do
know what you have to gain in this business. After all,
everyone knows that I myself named you private secretary
to His Majesty. You enjoy my trust. And although recently
you have obtained a certain power, I doubt that you were
sufficiently bold to think of conspiring to effect your own
reward. Is that not true?"

The confident smile was no longer as firm on the secretary's lips. "Naturally, Your Eminence," he said in a
low voice.

"And especially," Olivares continued, "not in matters involving foreign powers. Fray Emilio Bocanegra can emerge from this unscathed, since he is a man of the Church with influence at court. But it may cost others their heads."

As he spoke these words he threw a terrible and meaningful glance toward Alquézar.

"Your Eminence knows"—the royal secretary was nearly stuttering, and was again turning pale—"that I am completely loyal."

The minister's expression was one of profound irony. "Completely?"

"Yes, Your Eminence, that is what I said. Loyal. And useful."

"But let me remind you, don Luis, that I have cemeteries filled with 'completely' faithful and useful collaborators."

In his mouth, that pronouncement sounded even more dark and threatening. The Conde de Olivares picked up his quill with a distracted air, holding it as though preparing to sign a death sentence. Alatriste saw Alquézar follow the movement of the pen with agonized eyes.

"And now that we are speaking of cemeteries," the minister interjected suddenly, "I want you to meet Diego Alatriste, better known as Captain Alatriste. Have you met him?"

"No. I mean to say that, ahem . . . That I am not acquainted with him."

"That is the good thing about dealing with discreet parties. No one knows anyone."

Again Olivares seemed about to smile. Instead he pointed his quill toward the captain.

"Don Diego Alatriste," he said, "is an honorable man with an excellent military record—although a recent wound and bad fortunes have placed him in a delicate situation. He seems brave and trustworthy. . . . 'Solid' would be the proper term. There are not many men like him, and I am sure that with a little luck he will know better times. It would be a shame to find ourselves forever deprived of his potential services." He sent a penetrating glance toward the secretary to the king. "Do you not find that true, Alquézar?"

"Very true," the secretary hastened to confirm. "But with the kind of life that I imagine he leads, this Señor Alatriste exposes himself to many dangers. An accident, or something of the kind. No one can be responsible for that."

Having spoken, Alquézar directed an angry look at the captain.

"Oh, I can. I will be responsible," said the king's favorite, who seemed to be very comfortable with the direction the interview was taking. "And it would be well if on our parts we do nothing to precipitate such an unpleasant outcome. You do share my opinion, do you not, Señor Royal Secretary?"

"Oh absolutely, Your Eminence." Alquézar's voice was trembling with rage.

"It would be very painful for me."

"I understand."

"*Extremely* painful. Almost a personal affront."

Alquézar's contorted face suggested that bile was shooting through his system by the pint. The frightening grimace that distorted his mouth was intended to be a smile.

"Of c-course," he stammered.

The minister raised a finger, as if he had just recalled something, shuffled through the papers on the table, plucked out one of the documents, and handed it to the royal secretary.

"Perhaps it would add to your peace of mind if you yourself expedited this matter. This paper is signed by don Ambrosio de Spínola personally, and requests that don Diego Alatriste be paid four *escudos* for services in Flanders. That will, for a time, save him from having to draw his sword to earn a living. Do I make myself clear?"

Alquézar held the paper with the tips of his fingers, as if it were coated in poison. He looked toward the captain, wild-eyed, as though about to suffer a stroke. His teeth gritted with anger and spite.

"As clear as water, Your Eminence."

"Then you may return to your duties."

And without looking up from his papers, the most powerful man in Europe dismissed the secretary to the king with a wave of the hand.

When they were alone, Olivares looked up and held Captain Alatriste's eyes for a long moment. "I am not going to offer an explanation, nor do I have any reason to do so," he said gruffly.

"I have not asked an explanation of Your Excellency."

"Had you done so, you would be dead by now. Or on your way to being so."

Then silence. The king's favorite had risen to his feet and was walking toward the window, where he could see clouds threatening rain. He seemed to be concentrating on the guards in the courtyard. Hands crossed behind his back, standing against the light, he looked even more dark and forbidding.

"Whatever else," he said without turning, "you can thank God that you are still alive."

"It is true that it surprises me," Alatriste replied. "Especially after all I have just heard."

"Supposing that in fact you heard something."

"Supposing."

Still without turning, Olivares shrugged his powerful

shoulders. "You are alive simply because you do not deserve to die. At least not for the matter at hand. And also because there are those who have your interests at heart."

"I am grateful to them, Excellency."

"Do not be." The favorite moved away from the window, and his footsteps echoed on the parquet floor. "There is a third reason. There are those for whom your being alive is the gravest blow I can impose at this moment." He took a few more steps, nodding, pleased. "People who are useful to me because of their venality and ambition. But at times that same venality and ambition causes them to fall into the temptation of acting in their own behalf, or that of someone other than myself. What can one do? With upright men, one may win battles, perhaps, but not govern kingdoms. At least not this one."

He stood pensively regarding the portrait of the great Philip the Second above the fireplace; and after a very long pause he sighed deeply, sincerely. Then he seemed to remember the captain, and whirled toward him.

"As for any favor I may have done you," he said, "do not crow. Someone has just left this room who will never forgive you. Alquézar is one of those rare astute and complex Aragonese of the school of his predecessor, Antonio Pérez. His one known weakness is a niece of his, still a girl, a *menina* in the palace. Guard yourself against him as you would against the plague. And remember that if for a while my orders can keep him in line, I have no power at all over Fray Emilio Bocanegra. Were I in Captain Alatriste's place, I would quickly heal my wound and return to Flanders as soon as possible. Your former general, don Ambrosio de Spínola, is set to win more battles for us. It would be very considerate if you got yourself killed there, and not here."

Suddenly, Olivares seemed tired. He looked at the table strewn with papers as though in them he saw his condemnation, a long and fatiguing sentence. Slowly he sat down and faced them, but before he bade the captain farewell, he opened a secret door and took out a small ebony box.

"One last thing," he said. "There is an English traveler in Madrid who for some incomprehensible reason feels he is obligated to you. His path and yours, naturally, will in all probability never cross again. That is why he charged me to give this to you. Inside is a ring with his seal and a letter that—well, would you expect otherwise?—I have read. It is a kind of directive and bill of exchange that obliges any subject of His Britannic Majesty to lend aid to Captain Diego Alatriste should he ever have need. It is signed Charles, Prince of Wales."

Alatriste opened the black wood box with the ivory-inlaid lid. The ring was gold, and was engraved with the three plumes of the English heir. The letter was a small sheet folded four times, bearing the same seal as the ring, and written in English. When Alatriste looked up he saw that the favorite was watching him, and that between his ferocious beard and mustache gleamed a melancholy smile.

"What I would not give," said Olivares, "to have a letter like that."

EPILOGUE

The sky above the Alcázar threatened rain, and the heavy clouds blowing from the west seemed to rip apart on the pointed spire of the Torre Dorada. Sitting on a stone pillar on the royal esplanade, I covered my shoulders with the captain's old *herreruelo,* the short cape that served me for warmth, and continued to wait, never taking my eyes off the gates of the palace from which the sentinels had already chased me three times.

I had been there a very long while: ever since early morning, when I was roused from my uncomfortable dozing in front of the prison where we had spent the night—the captain inside and I out—and I had followed the carriage in which Constable Saldaña had driven the captain to the Alcázar and taken him in through a side gate. I had not eaten a bite since the night before, when don Francisco de Quevedo, before turning in—he had been recovering from a scratch suffered during the skirmish—came by the prison to inquire about the captain. When he found me huddled at the exit, he went to a nearby tavern and bought me a little bread and dried beef. The truth is, this seemed to be my destiny: a good part of my life with Captain Alatriste was spent waiting for him, expecting the worst. And always with my stomach empty and dread in my heart.

A cold drizzle began to moisten the large paving stones of the royal esplanade, little by little turning into a fine rain that drew a gray veil across the façades of nearby buildings and traced their reflections on the wet stones beneath my feet. I entertained myself by watching them take shape. That was what I was doing when I heard a little tune that sounded familiar to me, a kind of *ti-ri-tu, ta-ta*. Among the gray and ocher reflections stretched a dark, motionless stain. When I looked up, there before me, in cape and hat, was the unmistakable, somber figure of Gualterio Malatesta.

My first inclination when I saw my old acquaintance from the Gate of Lost Souls was to take to my feet, but I did not. Surprise left me so paralyzed and speechless that all I could do was sit there quietly, and not move, as the dark, gleaming eyes of the Italian nailed me to the spot. Afterward, when I could react, I had two specific and nearly opposite thoughts. One: Run. Two: Pull out the dagger I had hidden in the back of my waistband, covered by the cape, and try to bury it in our enemy's tripe. But something about him dissuaded me from doing either. Although he was as sinister and menacing as ever—lean, sunken-cheeked face marred by scars and pox marks—his attitude did not signal imminent danger. And in that instant, as if someone had swiped a line of white paint across his face, a smile appeared.

"Waiting for someone?"

I sat there on my stone pillar, staring at him. Drops of rain ran down my face, and rain collected on the broad brim of the Italian's felt hat and in the folds of his cape.

"I believe he will be coming out soon," he said in that muffled, hoarse voice, observing me all the while. I did not answer this time, either, and after a moment of silence, he looked over my shoulder and then all around, until his eyes settled on the façade of the palace.

"I was waiting for him, too," he added pensively, eyes now fixed on the palace gate. "For reasons different from yours, of course."

He seemed in a spell, almost amused by some aspect of the situation. "Different," he repeated.

A carriage passed. Its coachman was wrapped in a waxed cloth cape. I took a quick look to see whether I could make out the passenger. It was not the captain. At my side, the Italian was observing me again, that funereal smile still on his face.

"Have no fear. I have been told that he will come out on his own two feet. A free man."

"And how would you know that?"

My question coincided with a cautious movement of my hand toward the back of my waistband, a move that did not pass unnoticed by the Italian. His smile grew broader.

"Well," he said slowly. "I was waiting for him too. To give him a gift. But I have just been told that my gift is no longer necessary . . . at least for the moment. . . . They are releasing him *sine die.*"

The distrust on my face was so clear that the Italian burst out laughing, a laugh that sounded like wood splintering: crackling, coarse.

"I am going now, boy. I have things to do. But I want you to do me a favor. A message for Captain Alatriste. You will give it to him?"

I continued to watch him distrustfully, but did not say a word. Once more he looked over my shoulder, and then to either side, and I thought I heard him sigh very slowly, as if deep within. There, motionless, dressed all in black, beneath the rain that was steadily growing heavier, he too seemed tired. The thought flashed through my mind that perhaps evil men tire, just as loyal, feeling men do. After all, no one chooses his destiny.

"Tell your captain," said the Italian, "that Gualterio Malatesta has not forgotten that there is unfinished business between us. And that life is long—until it ends. Tell him, too, that we will meet again, and that on that occasion I hope to be more skillful than I have been till now, and kill him. With no heat or rancor, just calm, and with as much time as it takes. In addition to being a professional matter, this is personal. And as professional to professional, I am sure that he will understand perfectly. Will you give him the message?" Again that bright slash crossed his face, dangerous as a lightning bolt. "By my oath, you are a good lad."

He stood there, absorbed, staring at an indeterminate point in the shimmering gray reflections of the plaza. He made a move as if to leave, but stopped short.

"That other night," he added, still gazing toward the plaza, "at the Gate of Lost Souls, you did very well. Those point-blank pistol shots. *Dio mio.* I suppose that Alatriste must know that he owes you his life."

He shook the droplets of water from the folds of his cape and wrapped it tightly about him. His jet-black eyes finally stopped on me.

"I imagine that we will see each other again," he said, and began to walk away.

But after only a few steps, he turned back toward me. "Although, you know what I should do? I should finish you off now, while you are still a youngster. Before you become a man and kill *me*!"

Then he spun on his heel and walked away, once again the black shadow he had always been. And through the rain, I heard his laughter growing faint in the distance.

A SELECTION FROM

A POETRY BOUQUET

BY VARIOUS LIVELY MINDS

OF THIS CITY

Printed in the XVII century, lacking the printer's mark,
and conserved in the Nuevo Extremo
Ducal Archive and Library, Seville

In Praise of Military Virtue in the Person of Don Diego Alatriste

Sonnet

You, Diego, whose sword so nobly defends
The name and honor of your family,
As long as you are blessed with life to live,
You will battle every enemy.

You wear the tunic of an old brigade,
And with God's help, you wear it without stain.
Your scruples are so uncompromising
That you will never let it be profaned.

Courageous on the bloody battlefield,
In days of peace, still more honor you acquire.
And in your heart and mind there breathes such fire

That to empty boasting you will never yield.
In your faith and constancy you are so strong
You will embody virtue your whole life long.

On the Same Subject
in the Satiric Mode
Décima

In Flanders soil he drove a pike.
He drove even more, to wit,
He drove a Frenchman to take flight,
Screaming that he'd been badly hit.
Oh, he made a sorry sight.
Piteous how that man ran.
A foe may suddenly appear,
But I find I have naught to fear:
For in Ghent there is no better man
Than Alatriste, our brave *capitán*.

CONDE DE GUADALMEDINA

On the Sojourn of Charles, Prince of Wales, in Madrid

Sonnet

As he would win the fair infanta's hand,
The Prince of Wales came boldly to her land.
Whereon he found that such an enterprise
Is won not by the rash, but by the wise.

To win his suit, he swooped down one fine day,
Like an eagle, certain of his prey,
But found a troth, alas! will have no weight
When abrogated by affairs of state.

Thus Charles learned about diplomacy:
In the rough seas of the Spanish court
The most dauntless pilot may be brought up short.

As a dashing prince, similarly,
Will not wear upon his brow the wreath
Unless he persevere to his last breath.

FROM THE SAME HAND

To the Lord of La Torre de Juan Abad
with Similes from the Lives of the Saints
Rhymed octave

Behind good Roch, lame supplicant,

Behind Ignatius, chivalrous and valiant.

Behind Dominic, in combating a Protestant,

Behind John Chrysostom, so famously eloquent,

Behind Jerome, in learning and Jewish cant,

Behind Paul, the tactful and prudent,

Finally comes Quevedo, behind even Thomas,

And for every target, he brings his harquebus.

ABOUT THE AUTHOR

Arturo Pérez-Reverte lives near Madrid. Originally a war journalist, he now writes fiction full-time. His novels *The Flanders Panel*, *The Club Dumas*, *The Seville Communion*, *The Fencing Master*, *The Nautical Chart*, and *The Queen of the South* have been translated into twenty-eight languages and published in fifty countries. In 2003, he was elected to the Spanish Royal Academy.

Weidenfeld & Nicolson is proud to introduce
the remaining novels in the series
The Adventures of Captain Alatriste
by Arturo Pérez-Reverte:

Purity of Blood (January 2006)
The Sun over Breda (2007)
The King's Gold (2008)
The Caballero in the Yellow Doublet (2009)

Visit www.perez-reverte.com for excerpts
and other exclusive material.